ESCAPE FROM THE DEVIL
THE CROCKETTS' WESTERN SAGA: 9

ROBERT VAUGHAN

WOLFPACK
PUBLISHING
— EST 2013 —

WOLFPACK
PUBLISHING
— EST 2015 —

Published in the United States by Wolfpack Publishing, Las
Vegas

Wolfpack Publishing
6032 Wheat Penny Avenue
Las Vegas, NV 89122

wolfpackpublishing.com

Paperback ISBN 978-1-64734-252-4
eBook ISBN 978-1-64734-251-7

ESCAPE FROM THE DEVIL

Chapter One

Seven Rivers, New Mexico:

"Eight hundred dollars," Ernest Watters said. Watters owned the Rocking W ranch and the eight hundred dollars was the cost of ten quarter horses. Will and Gid Crockett bought the horses from Watters, because they had already contracted them to John Abernathy of the Long Trail Ranch, Reeves County, Texas, near the town of Toyah. Abernathy would be paying one hundred and sixty dollars for each horse, which would double their investment.

The task now, was to get the horses from Seven Rivers, New Mexico, to Toyah, Texas, a distance of three hundred miles.

"Why the hell don't they have a railroad running from here to Toyah?" Gid asked as they left the ranch with the ten horses.

"I guess there aren't enough people who want to go from Seven Rivers to Toyah," Will said with a little chuckle.

"Yeah, well, it'd sure make getting the horses to the colonel easier," Gid said. Gid referred to Abernathy as "Colonel" because that was the rank he had held in the Confederate army during the War Between the States and many still referred to him as such.

"It might be easier," Will agreed. "But it would probably cost two hundred dollars or so to rent the stock car. I think it's worth two hundred dollars for a ride of six days."

"I guess you're right. But herding horses isn't like herding cattle. When a horse thinks he's in danger, he just runs and only God knows where he'll wind up."

"That's true," Will said. "But there are only ten of them and if we can get just one of them to trust us, the others should follow along."

"You said this was gonna take six days. You think we can make fifty miles a day?"

"It's like you said, herding horses isn't like herding cattle. If we don't have anything to spook them, we'll be able to move them out at a pretty fast walk."

Will and Gid were still in New Mexico when they made camp the first night. It was an easy camp; there was water and graze for the horses and wood for the fire. They fried some ham steaks and potatoes and roasted a couple ears of corn. They had brought some beer with them and they were cooling a couple of bottles in the stream as they were preparing their meal.

"Three good things came from Missouri," Gid said. "Gid Crockett, Will Crockett and bottled beer from St Louis."

"Ha, I see you put your name first," Will teased.

"Well, yeah, but I put your name before the beer."

Will laughed. "I guess that's true."

They had had five days of easy herding and were now half-way through the sixth day. Will figured they would reach the ranch by mid-afternoon, but he wasn't aware of what they would encounter before they got there.

One mile ahead, Silas King and three men were waiting.

"I seen 'em early this morning," Rufus Taylor said. "They's ten horses, good lookin' horses they are too. Why, I bet we could get a thousand dollars for 'em just real easy."

"How many is bringin' 'em along?" King asked.

"They's only two of 'em."

"What do they look like?"

"They don't look like nothin'. Hell, they look like they'd run away scared if we just jumped out 'n said boo to 'em."

Silas King had a bushy head of very dark hair and a beard to match. But the most noticeable thing about him was his nose. At the Battle of Wilson's Creek, a Yankee officer made a slash across the bridge of his nose leaving a gash that separated the top half, from the bottom half, so that he looked as if he had two noses, one on top of the other.

"All right," King said. "You three get out there and wait for 'em. When they pass you by, kill 'em. Kill both of 'em. We don't want to be leavin' nobody to talk to the sheriff."

"How we goin' to do this?" Taylor asked. "I mean, we ain't got no place to hide, 'ceptin' here, 'n this is too far away."

"You don't need no place to hide. All you got to do is just stand out there like you was interested in just seein' the horses pass by. They won't expect nothin' just seein' you standin' there like that. You can even wave at 'em 'n pretend like you're just real interested. Then after they pass you by, draw your guns 'n shoot 'em. They won't be expectin' nothin' like that to happen, so killin' 'em will be easy as pie."

"All right," Taylor said. "Max, Clyde, let's get out there."

"Who the hell put you in charge?" Max asked.

"I did," King said.

"Well, if you say so, Boss, all right then."

"The horses is walking in pairs, so that they're five deep and two across. One man is ridin' on this side of 'em, 'n the other 'n is on the other side," Taylor said.

"Will?" Gid said as he and his brother were pushing the horses along at a brisk but comfortable pace. "You see those three men up there?"

"I do," Will replied.

"I've got me an itchy feeling about 'em. I don't know why anybody would just be standing there."

"Yeah, it's got me wondering too."

As Will and Gid continued to ride herd over the horses, one of the three men who was waiting ahead, waved and called out.

"Hey boys, them's sure some purty horses."

"Thank you," Will said.

"Got 'em sold, have you?"

"I think so."

"Too bad. I'd a bought one of them beauties in a heartbeat."

"I hope our buyer feels the same way," Gid said.

"Aw, you don't have to worry, any fool can see you've got some mighty good horseflesh there," one of the other men said as he came up to stand beside the other man.

"Well, these beauties as you call them, are almost home," Will said. "It was good talkin' to you."

The horses had barely cleared the three men when Will hesitated just a second, then he called out to Gid.

"Gid, watch where they go."

As Will and Gid turned, they saw the three men drawing their pistols, and even though he was mounted, Will was able to draw his gun and fire two quick shots and two men went down. Gid was able to shoot the third one. Neither of the three would-be horse thieves were able to get off a shot.

"We'd better see to them," Will said, and he and his brother walked back to check on the men who were lying on the ground.

"This one is still alive," Gid called over to his brother.

"Both of these men are dead," Will said. He walked over to see the one who was still alive. The would-be horse thief was gasping for breath and blood was coming from his mouth. No medical knowledge was needed to see that he would soon be dead. The wounded man's eyes darted back and forth, filled with fear and confusion.

"King," he said, the word barely audible.

"What?"

"King, Silas King. The son of a bitch just sent us out here to die."

The wounded man drew two more labored breaths, then died.

They reached Long Trail Ranch at about four o'clock that afternoon, where they were met by a man walking toward them, a smile on his face.

"Boy oh boy, if these are the horses, the Colonel is expecting, he's going to be some proud." the man said extending his hand. "Leo Hunter, I'm the foreman here at Long Trail."

"Glad to meet you, Leo. I'm Will Crockett and this is my brother, Gid." Will dismounted and shook hands. "We almost had an incident a couple of hours back, but we settled the matter. I expect these horses need some oats and water about now."

"I'll put them in the corral," Leo said. "Mr. Abernathy is up at the big house, but he's expecting you."

"As long as he has our money, we'll be happy to see him," Gid said.

Leo laughed. "I wouldn't worry about that. He can stand toe to toe with any man in Texas when it comes to his bank account."

"That's good to know," Gid said.

"This one is the leader," Will added, pointing to one of the horses.

Leo put a bridle on the horse Will had pointed out and started toward the corral. As he did so, the other horses fell in behind him.

"Well, well, well, I see you got here," someone said from behind their back and looking up they saw John Abernathy standing on the porch.

"Colonel," Will said giving a casual salute, and dipping his head.

"None of that, boys. This isn't Wilson Creek," Abernathy said referencing the battle where Will and Gid had been with him during the early part of the war.

"You've got quite a spread, here," Will said taking in the house and the outbuildings.

"Texas has been good to me," Abernathy said. "Come on in. I'm suspecting you may want to get your money, before Leo starts putting my brand on those horses."

"Will you do that right away?" Gid asked.

"You bet. There are horse thieves all over these parts and horse flesh that looks as good as the ones you brought up, would be easy pickings without a brand."

"I think we may have met a trio of those thieves about a half-day's ride back," Will said.

"Oh, dear. Did you get a chance to see any distinguishing markings on the horses, or the men for that matter? You need to tell the sheriff when you go back into town."

"As a matter of fact, we plan to do that," Will said. "Maybe he'll be able to recognize them, that is if the carrion haven't gotten to them before the sheriff gets there."

Abernathy shook his head. "Quantrill taught his raiders well. But, sometimes, you have no choice."

"I'd say when three men are planning on shooting us in the back and then running off with our horses, I'd say we shoot back," Gid said.

"*Our* horses? You mean my horses don't you?" Abernathy asked.

Will laughed. "Not yet, John. Until the cash is in our hands, they're still our horses, no matter how fast your man puts a brand on them."

"You said cash, I hope you'll accept a check, because I hate to have that much cash lying around out here," Abernathy said. "Even my hands know they're going to be paid by check. The word gets around and I think it spares me some headaches."

He handed an envelope to Will.

"Sixteen hundred dollars is a rather substantial check to present, so I've written a letter that you can show Mr. Montgomery, at the bank, if he should question you."

"Thanks."

"Now that our business is over, how about staying and having a bite to eat with Ethel and Julia and me? We get sort of hungry for conversation out here."

"We'd like to join you, Colonel, but I think we'd better go into town and see the sheriff. He needs to know about the three dead men we left back on the trail."

Abernathy nodded his head. "Yes, Sheriff Wallace will want to know about that."

John followed Will and Gid back out onto the front porch and just as they stepped out, a wagon full of boisterous children was coming up the long drive from the arch over the road that proclaimed this as the Long Trail Ranch.

Long Trail was a two hundred-thousand-acre cattle ranch which employed numerous cowhands. Seven of the men lived with their wives and children, in the little community of cabins that Abernathy provided. The foreman had his own private cabin, even though Leo Hunter wasn't married. The other five cowboys lived in the bunkhouse. Maria Arino, the cook and housekeeper, had her own room in the main house.

There were nine school-aged children who lived on the ranch and Mrs. Abernathy insisted that they be educated. They went to school in Toyah, which was seven miles away. These were the children who were in the wagon. On school days the sleepy children would leave before daybreak, Maria having provided a breakfast of biscuits and bacon. The driver would often spend the day in town tending to various errands that the foreman or either Mr. or Mrs. Abernathy had assigned to him. When the driver was finished, he picked up the children, whether the school day was over or not. It wasn't the best arrangement for the children, but Mrs. Abernathy accepted that what education they received, was better than none.

The colonel accepted this arrangement, mainly because it allowed his sixteen-year-old daughter to continue her education. The alternative was to send her to a boarding school back East somewhere, but he was reluctant to do that. From little on, Julia could have been described as a spirited child, and as she matured, she became more and more difficult to control. Even if it did mean, that he paid a hand to lollygag in town every day, it was his compromise to his wife.

Leo Hunter took over the task of assigning a driver and he rotated the duty around so that no one driver had to do it more than a week at a time.

"Look at that maniac, bringing that wagon in like he was a bat out of hell. If he hits a bump and one of those children gets tossed out, I'll have his hide," John said as he walked out to meet the wagon.

The driver pulled on the reins and brought the team to a stop.

"Sorry, Mr. Abernathy, but Julia always wants to go fast oncet we get to the lane," the driver said.

"Who do you take your orders from, Kincaid? Me or my daughter? Julia, get out of the wagon and that goes for the rest of you children as well. Get on home so you can help your mama with your chores."

"Yes, sir," many of the children said in unison as they jumped down from the wagon.

Only one person defied Mr. Abernathy and that would be who Will and Gid surmised to be his daughter. John had said she was sixteen, but she could have passed for someone much older. She was a beautiful girl burgeoning on womanhood and now she sat on the seat with the driver, her arm intertwined with his.

"Jamie, that was so much fun! You're the only driver I ever want to take us to school. Daddy, please say that Jamie will do this every day. You can tell Leo and he'll pick Jamie. Please, please, do it," Julia pleaded.

"Julia, go in the house and help your mother."

Julia purposefully, turned her attention to the driver. She patted him on the leg. "Don't worry, Jamie, I won't let Daddy yell at you. I'll see you tomorrow." She jumped down and passed by her father and Will and Gid without acknowledging anyone.

Will looked at John and saw the tightness of his jaw as he watched the interplay between his daughter and the driver of the wagon.

"Kincaid, get these horses rubbed down and put away. Don't let me ever see you mistreat these animals again, or you are out of a job, and. . . ." He did not complete his sentence.

Kincaid didn't answer, but he slapped the reins against the team and they started on.

"I'm sorry you had to witness that," John said. "Julia is a high strung, child, but Ethyl insists it's just her age. I guess we both love her too much for her own good."

"What do you think about that driver and the colonel's daughter?" Gid asked.

"Oh, I wouldn't think too much of it," Will said. "Little girls are always flirting with older men. I think it's part of growing up."

"Yeah, well, did you get a good look at her? I'm not sure you could call Julia a little girl," Gid replied. "Besides, wasn't Mama only sixteen when she married Papa?"

"Yes, but Papa was only nineteen. I don't think we can really make a comparison here. Kincaid appears to be nearly twice her age."

"From what I can see, the colonel is going to have his hands full," Gid said.

"You mean raising one little ole girl is harder than commanding five hundred men?" Will said. "I think the colonel is up to the job."

When the two brothers rode into Toyah, they saw that First Street was busy now, typical of those towns whose prosperity and growth was tied to the railroad. They rode down to the sheriff's office, then dismounted, looped the reins of their horses around the hitching rail, then went inside. There was a heavy-set man, wearing a badge, sitting at his desk playing solitaire.

"That's a good way to kill time," Will offered with a

smile.

"Yes, and you don't lose money playing it, the man replied."

"Sheriff Wallace?"

"I am, what can I do for you?"

"I'm Will Crockett, this is my brother Gid. We were bringing a string of horses up to Long Trail and we ran into a little trouble"

Sheriff Wallace cocked his head. "Would this have anything to do with three bodies Ned Cromwell brought in this morning?"

"If they were found about a half-day's ride from Abernathy's place, then yes, we are responsible," Will said.

Together, Will and Gid retold what had happened and how the three men had attempted to shoot them in the back.

"Did these men have any reason for killing you in particular, other than just stealing the horses?" Sheriff Wallace asked.

"Not that we know of," Gid said. "But I sort of got the idea that someone had been watching us, all along."

"Someone watching you, huh? Do you have any idea who that could have been?"

"One of the men said a name before he died. He didn't exactly say that he was watching, but he did indicate that he was involved."

"Do you remember the name?"

"King. Silas King."

"He's a bad one. It could have been King."

"Do you know him?" Will asked.

"Do I know him? No, not to talk to. But I sure know about him. He's been causing quite a bit of trouble around here, or least so people say. But we've never been able to directly connect him with anything he's being accused of."

"Believe me, sheriff, whatever he's accused of, he's guilty."

"You talk as if you know him."

"If he's the same Silas King we knew during the war, he's capable of doing anything," Will said. "Do people describe him as being one ugly son of a bitch?"

"As a matter of fact they do, say it's almost like he's got two noses."

Chapter Two

Because the bank was closed when they arrived in town, Will and Gid took a room in the Dunn Hotel. They took a bath, enjoyed a meal in the hotel restaurant and slept on beds for the first time in over a week. They started the next day rested and refreshed and after they cashed the check, they took a walk about town, just to check it out. There were two hotels, the Dunn and the Homestead. At least a score of businesses faced each other across Center Street.

"Will, how do you like this town?" Gid asked.

"I don't know. It's not much different than a dozen other towns we've gone through."

"What do you say we stay here for awhile? Maybe a month or two?" Gid suggested.

"Tired of traveling around, are you Little Brother?"

"Maybe. I don't want to put roots down here, but I

wouldn't mind staying for a little while. They have restaurants and bars. It might be good to eat some meals we didn't cook and play a little poker. Maybe strike up a conversation with a lady or two."

"All right, you talked me into it."

Gid chuckled. "I didn't have to talk very hard."

Thus it was, that after some years of wandering all around the West, the Crockett brothers called a temporary halt to their wanderlust and settled, at least for the time being, in the little town of Toyah, in Southwest Texas.

Will and Gid were impressed with the unspoiled panoramas and the isolated landscapes that seemed to be on a larger than life scale. Also, they knew for a fact that there were no wanted posters for them in Texas, because the governor had pardoned them. At one time they were wanted in Kansas, but they weren't sure for what but by now, even those circulars had been withdrawn. The wanted posters were not for any particular crime they had committed, but because they had ridden with Quantrill during the war.

As penance for what some called atrocities, Will and Gid Crockett made a conscious decision to do what they could to "right wrongs," whenever possible. Their reputation for good was spreading from one community to another and because of that they were seldom without a job.

After a few days in Toyah, Will and Gid were rested and rejuvenated, and when they walked into any establishment they were greeted as friends.

"Have we had enough?" Gid asked as they sat in a café finishing up their breakfast.

"You're full," Will said. "Are you sick? I don't believe I've ever heard those words from you before."

"No, I mean have we had enough of this town?" Gid asked. "It's nice and all that, but. . ."

"You're ready to move on," Will said.

"Mr. Crockett?" a young man said as he came toward the table. "I'm Danny Driscall and I drove the kids in to school today. Mr. Abernathy said if I found you, I was to give you this." He handed a note to Will.

"Thanks, Danny," Will said as he tore open the envelope.

"What's that about?" Gid asked.

"Sort of strange. Colonel Abernathy wants to hire us for a special job."

"Are we going to take it?" Gid asked.

"That depends on what the job is. It wouldn't hurt to augment our finances, since I do believe one of us has not been all that lucky at the poker table."

"Yeah," Gid replied. "You've got a point there."

* * *

When Will and Gid rode onto the sprawling ranch, they were met, personally, by Colonel John Abernathy himself.

"Thank you for answering my request that you come see me," John said. "You got here just in time for dinner."

Will smiled. "Gid is good about that."

There were five who were taking their meal at the dinner table that evening, Will and Gid were the guests, with their hosts, John and Ethyl Abernathy and their daughter.

The talk around the table was very cordial. Will and Gid told of their introduction to Toyah and the various experiences they had had in the little town, while John and Ethyl told of their recent trip to El Paso. During the whole meal, Julia had not made one comment.

"Well, I'll tell you this, young lady, it's not going to be too long before you'll be able to break some young man's heart," Will said in an attempt to bring Julia into the conversation.

"I already have a man, and I have no intention of breaking his heart," Julia said in a self-confident tone.

"Oh, someone at school?" Gid asked.

"I said I already have a *man* and he is certainly *not* a schoolboy," Julia said in a somewhat haughty tone. "Papa, may I be excused?"

"Perhaps that would be best, if you can't entertain us with a civil tongue," John replied.

Julia folded her napkin, then rose and walked away.

There was an awkward silence around the table for a moment or two, then John sighed.

"That is why I have asked you here," John said.

"You mean Julia?" Will replied, confused as to where this might be going.

"I've contacted my sister in Dominigo Springs, and she has agreed to let Julia come stay with her for a while. I think she needs a change of environment," John said as he let out a long sigh. "If you will agree to accompany her, I've bought passage for three on Friday morning's stage. It would be easier if the railroad went to Dominigo Springs, but it doesn't. Will you consider taking on the task?"

Will and Gid looked at each other as if questioning where this was going.

John smiled. "Obviously I don't expect you to go out of the goodness of your heart. I will give you two hundred fifty dollars apiece to see that Julia gets to my sister's safely."

"Five hundred dollars. That's a lot of money, just for the two of us to take a ride on the stage coach," Will said. "I have a feeling there may be more to this job, than to just to keep Julia company."

John nodded. "I'm glad you are that perceptive. It gives me a sense of confidence that I have chosen the right men for the job. Will, Gid, I'm sure that you have perceived that I am a very wealthy man. And because of that, I am concerned that someone might attempt to kidnap my daughter and hold her for ransom."

"Of course, if such a thing were to happen, I would not hesitate to pay whatever it took to get her back, but I wouldn't want that information to be known. Knowing what you may be confronting and I might add, knowing how difficult Julia can be, will you accept what I am offering?"

Again, the two brothers looked at each other and the nod they exchanged was perceptible only to them.

"All right, Colonel," Will said. "Surely, between the two of us we can see to it that Julia reaches Dominigo Springs safely."

"Thank you, thank you very much," a relieved John said as he shook the hands of both men. "I'll have her at the stage on Friday morning. I believe it's scheduled to leave at ten o'clock."

"*Perdóname por favor* Senor John, Senor Hunter is here to see you," a Mexican woman said, interrupting the conversation.

"Tell him I'll be right there, Maria," John said, then, to Will and Gid he added, "If you'll excuse me, I'll speak to Leo. You met him when you brought the horses. He's a good man and he knows more about cattle than anyone I've ever met."

"I just wish Mr. Hunter would find some good woman

to marry and then he would decide to stay here for good," Mrs. Abernathy said. "He does so much for John. I don't know what we would do without the man."

"I'm sure the colonel appreciates all that Mr. Hunter does for him," Will said. "Makes running a spread this large a lot easier."

"What do you think, Gid?" Will asked as they were riding back to the Toyah.

"Two hundred and fifty dollars just to ride a stage-coach? Sounds good to me," Gid said.

"You know there's more to it than that," Will said.

"You think he's trying to get her away from the fella that was driving the school wagon?" Gid asked. "I think he called him Kincaid."

"If I were guessing, I'd say that's what this is all about."

"What if she doesn't want to get away from him?"

"Five hundred dollars tells me she gets to the aunt's house in Dominigo Springs. What happens after that— that's anybody's guess," Will said.

On Friday morning when Will and Gid came down the stairs from their room, John and Julia were standing out front. The Dunn Hotel was the designated stop for the stagecoach.

"I don't want to visit Aunt Martha," Julia said, petulantly

"Why would you say something like that, Julia? You know your Aunt Martha loves you dearly."

"I don't want to go," Julia repeated.

Seeing Will and Gid, John turned to them and rolled his eyes. "Julia, have a seat on that bench over there. I need to talk to these two."

"I know what you're going to do—you're paying them to be my nursemaids," Julia said in a quarrelsome voice.

"It isn't any of your concern, young lady. This is between the Crocketts and me."

"What do you mean it isn't any of my concern? I'm the one who is being held prisoner here."

"Julia," John said in a voice which indicated he would take no more from her.

With what could only be described as a pout Julia walked over to take a seat.

John turned to Will and Gid with an expression of long-time suffering on his face. He sighed and shrugged his shoulders.

"You see what you will have to deal with," he said.

Will smiled. "She does seem to be a rather strong-willed young lady."

"That's an understatement and I'm afraid I've allowed it to happen. I know I should have reined her in years ago," John replied. "But when her sister died, it almost killed Ethyl. And after that . . ."

"We'll get her to your sister's safely, Colonel," Will said.

John nodded his head. "I'm satisfied that you will."

"Folks, here comes the coach!" someone shouted. "And Arthur's drivin'."

Will, Gid, John, and Julia waited while the team was changed on the coach. Arthur Sinclair ran into the hotel and came out with a bag of cinnamon rolls. When he saw the expression on Julia's face which was a cross between anger and defeat, he spoke to her.

"Girly, if you're goin' with me, I won't have no grumpin' on my coach. I was gonna ask ya if ya wanted to share my breakfast, but I ain't gonna waste no sugar on you."

"I'm not grumpy," Gid said.

Arthur laughed. "I guess you're not." He withdrew a bun and handed it to Gid. "Now, if you folks are goin' to Dominigo Springs, you need to climb aboard."

Will helped Julia aboard, then he and Gid climbed in behind her. They barely got the doors closed before the driver popped the whip with a report as loud as a pistol shot. The coach lurched forward.

No one spoke for about an hour. Gid ate his cinnamon roll and Will drew his hat down and sat quietly. Finally, Julia spoke.

"I heard Papa tell you, you're going with me for my protection, but I know he's just sending you along to keep an eye on me."

"That's probably true," Gid said.

"He said I should trust you, that he knew you during the war. Is that true?"

"Well, we did meet your pa at the battle of Wilson Creek before we joined up with . . ." Will stopped in mid-sentence. "Anyway, we met him, but he was a colonel, so it wasn't like we sat around a campfire drinking coffee with him."

Julia laughed.

"Ah, I see you can smile," Gid said. "You shouldn't have turned down Arthur's cinnamon bun."

"Miss Abernathy, what do you mean when you say we are to keep an eye on you?" Will asked.

"You know what he's doing. You saw how he treats me. He's sending me away so I can't be with Jamie."

"Jamie? That's Kincaid, the driver?" Gid asked.

"Yes, he's the most wonderful man in the world, and as soon as I get to Aunt Martha's I'm going to tell him where I am," Julia said. "He told me he would come for me and we'll get married."

"Are you sure that's what you want?" Gid continued.

"Of course it is. Jamie loves me and I love him. Papa doesn't like him because he's just a cowhand, but I think he's the most wonderful man in the world."

"How old is Jamie?" Will asked.

"He's thirty-two, but that doesn't make any difference."

Chapter Three

No more than fifteen miles west of Toyah, five men were waiting for the stage. They weren't waiting as passengers; their intention was much more sinister. The leader of the group was Silas King, a big man with dark hair and beard, and a nose-disfiguring scar. This handful of men was all that remained of the gang King had assembled. Of his original nine, three had been killed, and one had left to "scout for further opportunity".

"You reckon the coach will be carryin' any money?" one of the men asked.

"It might be carryin' some, but that ain't the reason we'll be stoppin' it," King said.

"Yeah, I know, you said we're stoppin' it so's we can take the girl, but how do we know this girl's even on the stage, anyway?"

"I know she's on the stage and that's all that matters,"

King said, cryptically.

"I hear it coming," one of the others said.

"Get ready," King ordered.

King and the others were behind some trees where the road curved, so that they were hidden from the driver of the approaching coach. Then, just as the coach came around the curve, they rode out into the road, blocking the way. The driver pulled the coach to an abrupt stop.

"Here, what are you . . ." the driver started, but that was as far as he got before three shots were fired.

Inside the coach, Will and Gid were put on alert, first by the unexpected stop, then, the gunshots. Will reached out to Julia.

"Get down on the floor!" he ordered and, frightened, Julia did as she was told.

Will jumped out of the coach on the left side, while Gid exited the other side.

"What the hell?" one of the men who had stopped the coach shouted. He fired at Will but missed. Will returned fire and didn't miss. For the next few seconds there was a spirited exchange of gunfire which stopped, only when all four of the men were down.

King had been standing to one side of the road when his men killed the driver, but when the return shooting started, he backed away, putting some distance between himself and the others. Then, toward the end of the firing, King began shooting as well, but instead of shooting at Will or Gid, he was shooting at his own men.

When the last shot was fired, King looked over at the two men who had exited the stage.

"It looks like we got 'em all," King said.

"I'll be damn. Silas King," Will said.

King squinted at Will as if trying to recollect who it might be, then recognition crossed his face. "You two are the Crockett brothers, ain't ya'? Well, I guess it was good that you two was on the coach, 'cause I'm not sure I could've handled all four of 'em by my ownself."

"What do you mean, handle them by yourself?"

"I come along just as the driver was shot, 'n I figured to do what I could to help out. Then you two boys come out. Well, I remember you from when we rode together with Quantrill. You two always was good men."

"Drop the gun, King, it won't work," Will said.

"What are you talking about?"

"You weren't trying to stop these men, you were part of them, just the way you were part of the men who tried to steal our horses. Now, drop the gun."

"You're makin' a mistake," King said.

"I'm not telling you again. Drop the gun, or I'll shoot you where you stand," Will ordered.

King dropped the gun, then put his hands up.

"Look here, is this any way to treat someone who rode side by side with you durin' the war. We was friends then."

"We were never friends, King. Gid, get a shoelace from one of those men, and tie King's thumbs together behind his back."

A few minutes later, Will helped King into the coach and had him sit on the seat across from Julia.

"I'm scared," Julia said in a frightened voice.

"Nothing to be afraid of now; he can't hurt you," Will said, as he took a seat beside her. "I'm sorry for the intrusion, Miss Abernathy. But this is the only way I know to get him back."

"Back?"

"We're returning to Toyah."

"No, we're going to Dominigo Springs," Julia said.

"Not now, we're not."

"What about your brother? Where is he? Was he...shot?"

"He's driving."

"What about Mr. Sinclair? Why isn't he driving?"

"Because he is dead."

"Oh, my," Julia said, putting her hand to her mouth.

"Look, Miss, I didn't have nothin' to do with this," King said. "All I done was try 'n stop them four men from snatchin' you up so as to get any money from your pa."

"How did you know that?" Will asked.

"How did I know what?"

"How did you know that they were after Julia? What made you think they weren't just wanting to rob the coach?"

The expression on King's face showed that he had made a major mistake.

"I don't know," he mumbled. "I just sort of guessed."

"We'll just see how that goes over with the judge."

The citizens of Toyah who watched the coach come into town from the same direction it had left less than two hours earlier, were surprised to see it. They were more surprised to see that it wasn't being driven by Sinclair, and even more surprised when it stopped, not at the Dunn Hotel, but at the city jail.

Will hopped down with the prisoner, then called up to Gid.

"Get the coach and the driver on down to the livery, then wait with the girl. We'll take her back to her pa."

"I'll be damn," Sheriff Wallace said, coming out to meet the coach. "I do believe this must be Silas King. Come on in, Mr. King, I have a nice cell all picked out for you."

"I didn't do nothin' but try 'n stop what was goin' on. I was on the girl's side 'n I near bout had it took care of myself, a'fore the Crocketts jumped out of the coach and got the drop on me."

"No need in tellin' me about it, save your story for the court," Sheriff Wallace said. "Come on, get in there." Wallace punctuated his order by waving a pistol in King's face, to enforce his demand.

The livery man made arrangements with the mortician to take care of Sinclair's body, then unhitched the horses and stored the stagecoach. Nothing else could be done, until the next stage made a run.

Will and Gid rented a surrey and took Julia back to the Long Trail Ranch. When they pulled up in front of the Abernathy big house, Leo Hunter met the surrey.

"What are you doing back? And with Julia? Is something wrong?" Hunter asked.

"I'd say," Will said. "We had a bit of a problem."

At that moment, without being summoned, John and Ethyl came out to meet them, showing their concern by the expressions on their faces.

"What has happened?" John asked. "Julia, why aren't you on the coach to Dominigo Springs?"

"Oh, Papa, it was awful!" Julia said as she jumped down from the surrey. "Will and Gid saved my life. I'm not just saying that—they really did." She hurried over to throw herself into her mother's arms.

Upon seeing the unexpected return of the Crocketts and Julia, the hands who were around the place came over to see what had happened.

Jamie Kincaid was among them. He moved over to stand beside Julia and her mother. "Honey, are you all right? What happened?"

Ethyl Abernathy bristled when she heard Kincaid call her daughter "honey," and she shifted her body to shield Julia from the man.

"Oh, Jamie, I've never been so frightened in my life, but Will and Gid saved me."

"Come on in and tell me exactly what happened," John said as he ushered his wife and daughter toward the house.

Will told the story in every minute detail, including Silas King making a bogus claim that he was there to help.

"So, you don't believe King's explanation?" John asked.

"I would just as easily believe that the moon is made of cheese," Will replied. "Sherriff Wallace says he'll get his chance to tell it to court, because I expect they'll be having Mr. Silas King's trial soon. Oh and Colonel, I'm sure they'll want Julia to testify."

"How do you feel about that, Sweetheart?" John asked his daughter. "Do you feel you'll be able to testify?"

"I want to testify, Papa. I want to see that ugly man go to jail."

"Well, you two men didn't get my daughter delivered to Dominigo Springs, but you certainly did earn your money. Come on into my study and I'll pay you the rest of it."

Julia went to her room telling her mother she was exhausted and that she wanted to change out of her traveling dress, and then rest for a while. What she really wanted to do was sneak out of the house and find Jamie.

She found him near the corral.

"Did you miss me, Jamie?" Julia asked flirtatiously.

"Ha, how could I miss you? You weren't gone more'n half a day," Kincaid replied with a teasing smile. He pulled her to him and then guided her behind the shed.

"But if I had gone to my aunt's house for a long time like papa wanted, you would have missed me, wouldn't you?"

"No, because I would have come to get you, and I would have carried you off like a white knight in shining armor," Kincaid said, laughing.

"I know you're teasing now," Julia said. "But I know if those men had taken me, I really do think you would have come to rescue me."

"You know I'd be there, Julia, but right now, you'd better be scootin' on back to the house. If your pa finds out you come out to find me, who knows what he'll do."

"I'll go, Jamie, but I'll see you tomorrow. I'm going to dream about you all night." Julia reached up and kissed him. "I'm so glad I'm home again."

"Now, I mean it. Get out of here," Jamie said, but as he did so, he gave her a playful swat on the behind.

Julia giggled as she ran toward the back of the house.

Leo Hunter was in the barn and he overheard the interplay between Julia and Kincaid and after Julia went back into the house, he walked around the shed to talk to him.

"Kincaid, you need to leave that little girl alone."

"Look here, Hunter, you might be the foreman, 'n you can tell me what calf to brand or what cow to rope, but you ain't got no right tellin' me what woman I can talk to."

"That's just it. Miss Abernathy isn't a woman, she's a young girl and if you keep sniffing around her, there's going to be trouble."

"Yeah? Well it ain't none o' your business." Kincaid turned and walked toward the bunkhouse.

* * *

"I suppose she told you all about Kincaid," John said as he opened a drawer on his desk and pulled out a packet of money. He began counting off what he owed them.

"She did mention him," Will said. "If I were to comment, I'd say she thinks pretty highly of him."

"She's sixteen and he's thirty-two," John said. "He's twice her age."

"Why haven't you fired him?" Gid asked.

John sighed. "First of all, I'm a little short-handed right now and firing him would put more work on poor Leo. But the main reason he's still here, is because as nearly as I can determine this has all been Julia's doing. Even though she has some young girl's attraction to him, from what I have observed, he's never done anything to encourage it, except be nice to her. I can't very well fire him for something that isn't his fault."

Chapter Four

The first thing Will and Gid did after they returned the surrey to the livery, was visit the Broke Cowboy Saloon for a beer. By now it was late enough in the day that there were already several customers present, but there were a few empty tables, so they took their beers to one of them. As soon as they sat down, they were joined by Mert and Rosanna, two of the bar girls that they knew from their previous visits.

"Why, if it isn't the two most handsome men in all of Texas," Mert said with a broad smile.

"What do you mean two?" Gid asked. "Surely, you aren't including this old man, are you? Why, he's one of the ugliest men I've ever seen and the only reason I let him hang around me is because he's my brother."

Rosanna laughed. "Why, Gid, don't you know the only reason we come over to see you is because Will's so handsome."

"Well, if you people are finished with all this foolish talk, maybe you ladies would like to have a drink with us," Will invited.

"I'll get them," Mert said, starting toward the bar.

"Is it true," Rosanna asked when the women were seated, "that you two brought in Silas King?"

"Yes. Do you know him?" Will asked.

"No, I don't know him, but I've heard of him. Just about everyone in these parts has heard somethin' about him."

"The talk is he wanted to take Julia Abernathy off the stagecoach," Mert said.

"That's what he'll be charged with," Will said.

"Too bad he didn't get the job done," Mert said.

"What?" Gid asked, surprised by Mert's comment. "You don't really mean that, do you?"

"No, not really," Mert said. "It's just that she's such an arrogant little twit who thinks she's better than everyone else, but not even she deserves to be kidnapped I guess. What Jamie Kincaid sees in her; I'll never know."

"Wait a minute, are you saying there really is something between Jamie Kincaid and Julia?" Will asked, surprised to hear Mert say that.

"Not really," Rosanna said. "At least not from Kincaid's side. I think he's flattered, but that's all."

"You know Kincaid?" Will asked.

"Oh, honey, every girl in here knows Kincaid."

Mert laughed. "That's one thing you can say about him, he believes in one for all."

"Will, there's Deputy Parsons. Is he looking for you two?"

Glancing toward the front door, Will saw the deputy looking around the room as if searching for someone.

"I'll go see if we're the ones he's after," Gid said, getting up from the table.

Half-way between the table and the front door, the deputy saw Gid and started walking toward him.

"There you are. The sheriff wants to see you and Will."

Five minutes later, Will, Gid, Sheriff Wallace and the prosecutor, Tony Murchison, were meeting in the sheriff's office. Murchison was a man of average height, with sandy hair and a spray of freckles.

"You gentlemen will be my witnesses for the prosecution," Murchison said. "So, if you don't mind, I'd like for you to tell me in your own words what happened."

Will and Gid began talking, first one, then the other, until the full story was told.

Murchison sighed and shook his head. "So neither one of you actually saw King with the others?"

"No."

"This is going to be a difficult case to make. Without your testimony, there will be little to disprove his allegation that he wasn't a part of it, but had only happened onto the stagecoach while the holdup was in progress."

"What stagecoach holdup?" Will said with a smile. "They weren't after money, they were after Julia and King knew it."

The Trial

"All rise for His Honor, Judge Alan Briggs!" the bailiff shouted.

Those present in the court room stood as a rather heavy-set man, bald and wearing rimless glasses, came into the room. He took his seat behind the bench.

"You may be seated," the bailiff said.

With the arrival of the judge, those who were present would now be referred to as the gallery and the gallery was seated.

"Mr. Bailiff, for what purpose have we convened?" Judge Briggs asked.

"Your Honor, comes now the state of Texas and the defendant, Silas King," the bailiff said.

"Is attorney for Texas present?" Judge Briggs asked.

The prosecutor stood. "Tony Murchison for the prosecution, Your Honor."

"Is the defendant represented by counsel?"

"David Vernon, for the defense, Your Honor," Vernon

responded.

"In the case of Texas verses Silas King, this court is now in order. Prosecution, you may make your case," Judge Briggs said.

Tony Murchison stood. "Your Honor, if it please the court, prosecution calls Gideon Crockett to the stand."

After being sworn in, Gid took his seat, and Murchison began with the state's case against Silas King. "Mr. Crockett, where were you on the eighth of April?"

"My brother and I were on our way to Dominigo Springs."

"You say you were on your way. What was your means of conveyance?"

"We were going by stagecoach."

"And did anything of any particular interest happen while the coach was in route?"

"Our coach was attacked by five armed men," Gid said.

"And do you see any of those men in this courtroom?"

"Yes, sir, I do."

"Would you point him out and identify him to the court, please," Murchison said.

Gid pointed to the defendant. "That man, Silas King."

"Are you certain that this is the man you saw?"

"Oh, yeah," Gid said. "I'm absolutely certain."

"Your witness, counselor," Murchison said as he returned to the prosecutor's table.

Attorney for Defense, David Vernon, was a large man with a bulging neck and multiple chins. He was bald on top of his head, but he had a line of hair that encircled his head, then connected to bushy sideburns, that ended with a full moustache.

Vernon approached the witness stand, then stood there for just a moment, fixing Gid with a steely stare.

"You have testified that Mr. King held up the stage, is that right."

"That's right."

"What money did he take?"

"What?"

"You said he held up the stage, what money did he take? Did the stage have a strong box? If so, did Mr. King take the strong box?"

"No, he didn't get the strong box."

"I see. So he robbed the individual passengers, is that it?"

"No, he didn't get any money from the passengers, either."

"He got no money from the strong box and no money from the passengers, and yet you have just testified that he robbed the stage. I'm sure you can understand my confusion."

"Well he was going to take ..." Gid started, but he was interrupted by the raised hand of counsel for the defense.

"Your Honor, please inform the witness to speak only in response to my questions."

"Mr. Crockett, add no comment which does not constitute an answer to a direct question," Judge Briggs said.

"Thank you, Your Honor," Vernon said. "I have no further questions for this witness."

"Your Honor, prosecution calls William Crockett."

As Gid was before him, Will was sworn in, then took his place in the witness chair. Will's account of the events that transpired mirrored those of his brother.

"Mr. Crockett, why were you and your brother on the stagecoach?"

"We were being paid by Mr. John Abernathy to see that his daughter made the trip to Dominigo Springs safely."

"Was Miss Abernathy on the stagecoach when Silas King stopped the stage?"

"She was."

"Is Mr. Abernathy a wealthy man?"

Will chuckled. "He's rich as Croesus."

There was a scattering of laughter, and though Judge Briggs didn't find it necessary to gavel down, he did fix a disapproving glare upon the gallery.

"Mr. Crockett, is it possible that Miss Abernathy might have been the target, rather than a robbery? Perhaps to be held for ransom?"

"I am absolutely certain that she was the target."

"Your witness, counselor," Murchison said, turning away from Will.

"The court will take a brief recess," Judge Briggs announced.

Chapter Five

During the recess Will, Gid and Julia met with Murchison
in a small meeting room off the gallery.

"Miss Abernathy, you'll be next. I'll call you to the
stand after defense finishes with Mr. Crockett. We've
already discussed what my questions will be, but when
the lawyer for the defense starts in on you, there is no
telling what he might ask.

"But if I don't call you as a witness, he won't be able to
ask you anything. So, it's your choice. Do I call you, or not?"

"Call me, I want to testify," Julia insisted.

Murchison nodded. "Good for you, young lady. I'll call
you right after defense gets through with Will."

The court clerk stuck his head in through the door.
"Court is about to start up again."

Will, Gid, Julia and the prosecutor returned to their
positions in the front row of the gallery.

"Court is now in session. Mr. Vernon, do you intend to cross examine Mr. William Crockett?"

"I do, Your Honor."

"Mr. Crockett, kindly retake the stand and remember that you have already been sworn in."

With a nod, Will retook the stand and looked over at the defense table, where Vernon was shuffling papers around.

"Mr. Vernon, please carry on, or forfeit the session," Judge Briggs ordered.

Vernon approached the witness. "Mr. Crockett, how many people attacked the coach?"

"Five."

"Five people attacked the stage, and yet you brought in only one. Where are the other four attackers?"

"They are dead."

"Dead?"

"Yes, my brother and I killed them."

"You say five men attacked the coach and you killed four of them? Why didn't you kill the fifth man?"

"Because he wasn't with them."

"Ah ha!" Vernon held up his finger, then turned to the jury. *"Because he wasn't with them,"* he said, in a dramatic repeat of Will's response to his question.

"Oh, he was there, all right," Will said, resolutely. "We didn't see him until after it was all over."

Vernon continued his cross examination, playing hard upon Will's comment that "King wasn't with them," but he was unable to make any inroads into Will's testimony.

"Your honor, I have no further questions of this witness."

When Will was returning to his seat, Murchison stood up. "Your Honor, the state calls Miss Julia Abernathy."

Julia walked up to the witness stand, raised her hand and was sworn in.

"Miss Abernathy, would you tell the court, in your own words, what happened on the tenth of this month," Murchison said.

"I was on the coach on the way to visit my Aunt Martha when those awful men attacked the coach, Will and Gid kept them from taking me away."

"Why, do you suppose, would they want to take you?"

"Because my father has money. I think they wanted to take me and keep me as their prisoner until my father paid them money to let me go."

"Is your father well known?"

"Yes, I think so."

"So, it's not hard to believe that the men who attacked the stagecoach knew your father had money."

"I'm sure they did know."

"Miss Abernathy, think before you answer this question, because this is the very crux of this examination. Did the defendant speak to you when he got into the coach?"

"Yes, sir, he did."

"And, what did the defendant say to you?"

"He said, 'All I done was try 'n stop them four men from snatchin' you up so as to get any money from your pa'."

"Thank you, Miss Abernathy." Murchison turned toward the defense table. "Your witness, counselor."

"Miss Abernathy, did you actually see Mr. King with the men who were attacking the coach?" Vernon asked.

"No, sir."

"In fact, Miss Abernathy, you didn't see any of them, did you?"

"No, sir."

"Why didn't you see any of them?"

"Because Will told me to get down on the floor of the coach until it was all over."

"Were you frightened?"

"Yes, sir, I was very frightened."

"How long were you lying on the floor?"

"Until Will came back to the coach with Mr. King."

"Is that the first you knew that it was all over?"

"Yes, sir."

"You testified that Mr. King told you that he was trying to keep you from, 'being snatched up,' I think you said. Isn't it possible that you didn't hear that directly from him, but that you heard Will Crockett tell you that's what

Mr. King said? If that is how it happened, then you aren't providing us with direct evidence; you are providing us with heresay evidence and that isn't admissible."

"No, sir, I heard Mr. King say it," Julia insisted.

"By your own admission you said you were lying on the floor and you were terrified. I think it is very possible that you mis-remembered."

"I heard Mr. King say that." Julia insisted.

Vernon stared at her for a long moment, so long that Julia began to feel very uncomfortable.

"No further questions," Vernon said, returning to the defense table.

"Mr. Vernon, are you ready to present your summation to the jury?"

"I am, Your Honor."

Vernon walked over to the jury box. "How many of you fought on the side of the Confederacy during our late unpleasantness?

Eight of the jurors raised their hands.

"That leaves four of you who did not fight for the South. Did any of you four fight for the North?"

No one raised their hand.

"I want you to look at the defendant. And I, especially want you to look at his nose. It is badly disfigured, so badly so that Mr. King must bear the weight of knowing he will never have a face that would appeal to the ladies and has even been known to frighten little children.

Vernon paused before his next sentence. "He looks like that, because at the Battle of Wilson's Creek, the saber of a Yankee officer cut his nose so that it looks as if he has two noses, one on top of the other."

"But let's get to this spurious charge against my client. By their own admission, not one of the three witnesses who testified for the prosecution actually saw Mr. King with the men who attacked the coach."

"Mr. King, asserts that he was there in defense of the coach. There is no proof that he wasn't there to help the stagecoach driver. Now, here is an interesting fact for you. Both of the Crocketts use .44 caliber pistols, but there are three .36 caliber rounds the coroner found in the body of Amos Garland. Silas King was carrying a .36 caliber pistol." Vernon looked toward the judge. "Defense rests, Your Honor."

Murchison approached the jury box. "Let's examine this case logically," he began. "Silas King was a wanted man before the incident with the stagecoach that is the subject of this trial."

"Does it seem logical that a wanted man would just happen onto a stagecoach holdup and decide to risk his life against four men, to come to the aid of the stagecoach?"

"You heard Miss Abernathy testify that King said that he was just trying to prevent her from being kidnapped?"

"Does it seem logical that someone who just happened onto four men shooting at the stagecoach would know that their target was the young lady in the coach and not any money the coach might be carrying?"

"As counselor for the defense, Mr. Vernon pointed out that there were three .36 caliber rounds in Garland's body. But those three rounds were blood free, meaning they were postmortem. Would it not be logical to assume that if King wanted to make the case that he was there to help the stagecoach passengers, that he might shoot into the body of one of his own, already dead, men to strengthen his case?"

"Using logic, presented evidence and intelligence, one can easily surmount any doubt as to Silas King's guilt. And I ask that you find him so."

The jury retired for deliberation but returned before the courtroom had even been cleared. Judge Briggs gaveled the court in order, then addressed the jury.

"Have you reached a verdict?

"We have, Your Honor."

"And what is that verdict?"

"Your honor, we find the defendant, Silas King guilty as charged."

Chapter Six

Will and Gid were with Tony Murchison in the Neighborhood Café. All three of the Abernathys came in and joined them at the table in the corner.

"I have to say thank you to all three of you," John said as he pulled out a chair for Ethyl.

"Yes," Ethyl said. "I must say I was a bit concerned when Vernon talked about the bullets. I thought King would go free."

"It was a good thing you had examined those bullets, Tony," John said.

Murchison smiled. "That's what you pay me for."

"You got him put away for twenty years," John said. "That's good enough for him."

"I'm just sorry we couldn't get the judge to hang him," Gid said.

"You knew him during the war?" Murchison asked.

"Yes, for a while, we rode with him in . . . our unit," Gid said.

"And never have I met a more debauched human being," Will added.

"Well, he's going to be away for a long time. He won't be bothering anyone else," Murchison said.

"I wish I could be as confident," Will replied.

The next day John invited Will and Gid for dinner.

The main house was at least a quarter of a mile from the gate and when they reached it, they rode up the curved driveway to be met by Danny Driscoll, the young man who had delivered the colonel's message.

"Howdy, Mr. Crockett and Mr. Crockett" he said. "Do you want me to take care of your horses?"

"Thanks, Danny," Will said as he dismounted. "If you'd rub them both down, there's a quarter in it for you."

"Yes, sir, these two horses'll have the best rubdown they've ever had."

The brothers stepped up onto the porch where they were met by John Abernathy and greeted by the delicious aroma of roasting beef.

"Welcome back. I'm glad you boys could come to our little celebration," John said.

"Colonel, there was never any doubt but that we would

be here," Will said. "There's no way we would turn down a home-cooked meal."

John chuckled. "Whatever it takes to get you here," he said.

After Ethyl greeted them, she returned to the kitchen to supervise the preparation of the meal. John invited Will and Gid into the drawing room.

"Gentlemen, I have something to give you—a check for twelve hundred fifty dollars. I'm sure you will be able to make an equitable division between the two of you."

Will held up his hand as if refusing the offer. "Colonel, as tempting as that is, I see no reason for you to be paying us more. You've already paid us the agreed upon amount we were told we would get."

John chuckled. "Oh, good heavens, boys, you misunderstand. This isn't my money; it comes from the state of Texas."

"The state?" Gid asked.

"Yes. There was a twelve hundred and fifty dollar reward offered for the capture of one Silas King and Sheriff Wallace put in for it to be payable to you two."

"Well now, if it isn't coming from you, we'll be happy to take it," Will said.

John laughed. "I thought you might."

* * *

Leo Hunter was in the barn when he heard what he thought was a woman's voice. He listened thinking it may have been Julia, but as no word had been spoken he wasn't sure.

Continuing to investigate, Hunter quietly climbed the board ladder to look into the loft. He saw Kincaid and Julia together. Kincaid was kissing her, but there was more to it than that. Kincaid had his hand on the girl's bare breast.

For a moment, Hunter was unsure of what he should do. Should he call out to Kincaid? He was the foreman and he had every right to do so, but Julia was the boss's daughter. In that moment, he knew what he had to do.

John was laughing at something Gid had just said when he heard the knock on the door. He wasn't expecting anyone and he knew that none of his hands would come to the house at this hour, especially when he was entertaining. Unless it was important.

"Excuse me, gentlemen," he said as he rose. "Now don't start another story until I get back."

Will and Gid could hear the sound of a man talking, but he was talking so quietly that they couldn't make out what he was saying.

"WHAT?" John's response was so loud that it was almost a scream. He turned away from the still open door.

"Colonel, what is it?" Will asked.

"I'm going to get my gun!" John said.

"What is happening? Why do you need a gun?"

"Because I'm going to kill that son of a bitch!"

"Who are you going to kill?"

"I'm going to kill Kincaid. That son of a bitch is in the hayloft with my daughter."

Will stuck his hand out to stop John.

"Colonel, you don't need to kill him. Just fire him and order him off your ranch."

"I'm not sure he would go," John said. "I need my gun."

"You don't need a gun, Colonel, as long as you have us. Come on, we'll take care of this situation together."

Hunter led the three men out to the barn, then pointed up to the loft.

"Leo, what is . . ." that was as far as John got, before they heard something that sounded like a woman's moan. It came from above.

Quickly John, Will and Gid climbed the ladder to the loft. There, lying in a pile of hay, they saw Kincaid and Julia. Julia was still in her dress, but the bodice was opened, and her shoulders were bare. Kincaid had one hand on a breast, while the other was bunching her dress up to her waist. They were so involved with each other, that neither of them saw the three men as they approached.

"Kincaid, you son of a bitch! Get the hell off my ranch

and don't you ever step foot on my land again!"

"Papa!" Julia squealed in fear and embarrassment. She clutched her bodice closed.

"You got no right to talk to me like that," Kincaid said.

Will cocked his pistol, the sound of the hammer coming back loud in the stillness of the loft.

"I would say that he does," Will said.

"Girl, get in the house, now," John said.

Crying from anger, resentment and embarrassment, Julia hurried down the ladder and ran across the back yard to the house.

Leo Hunter led a subdued and frightened Kincaid into the bunkhouse to get his tack.

"He has no right to do this to me," Kincaid said.

"Kincaid, I told you to stay away from that little girl. You're damn lucky the Crocketts were here, or Colonel Abernathy would have shot you. If it had been my daughter, that's what I would have done."

Will, Gid, and John were standing on the porch, watching as a disgruntled Jamie Kincaid rode away.

"I expect dinner is on the table now," John said.

"Colonel, under the circumstances, I think you and your family might need a little time alone," Will said.

John nodded. "Regretfully, that may be so."

"As we ride into town, we'll make certain that Kincaid doesn't circle around and try and come back," Gid said.

"Gentlemen, I can't tell you how much I value and appreciate your friendship," John said.

Less than two miles from the entry gate to Long Trail Ranch, Will and Gid saw a rider, sitting on his horse, just off the side of the road. At first, he was too far away to be identified. Gid recognized him first.

"It's that son of a bitch Kincaid. I wonder what he's doing here?"

"Whatever it is, you can be sure he's up to no good," Will replied.

The brothers thought Kincaid would ride away when he saw them, but defiantly, he stayed where he was until the distance between them was closed.

"What are you doing here, Kincaid?" Will asked.

"It ain't none o' your business what I'm doin' here," Kincaid replied. "I'm ridin' on a public road."

"No, you aren't," Will said. "You're just sitting here, and that makes me wonder why?"

"I'm resting my horse."

"He's rested now. Why don't you come on into town with us?" Will managed a smile. "Gid will buy you a drink. Won't you, Gid?"

"What? Why do I have to buy the son of a bitch a drink?"

"Because you are a good man, and you want to be nice,"

Will replied.

"All right, I'll buy the drinks."

"Come on, Kincaid, how can you turn down a free drink?"

Kincaid nodded. "All right, I'll come with you."

"What do you want?" Gid asked when they dismounted in front of the Broke Cowboy Saloon.

"Whiskey," Kincaid said.

Once inside, Gid made the purchase, then, with drinks in hand, two beers and one whiskey, the three men found a table.

"Kincaid, what were you doing messing around with the Colonel's daughter? You knew damn well that was going to get you in trouble," Will said.

"She kept comin' after me," Kincaid said. "She's a good lookin' woman, I'm a man, what was I supposed to do?"

"Well now, you see, there's your problem. She isn't a woman yet; she is still a young girl. She's only sixteen for crying out loud."

"She might be only sixteen, but she sure don't look sixteen. Why, she's shaped up as good as any woman I've ever seen. And like I told you, she was comin' after me."

Rosanna came over to join them, wearing a broad, practiced smile, and a blouse that gave everyone a very good look.

"Jamie, what brings you here so early, and the middle of the week? Does the Colonel know you're here?"

"Yeah, he knows," Kincaid replied.

"Well, whatever the reason is, I'm glad you're here." Rosanna put her hand on his shoulder. "Last time you went upstairs with Mert. It's my time now."

"Yeah," Kincaid said, finishing his drink and setting the empty glass on the table. "That might be just what I need right now."

Will and Gid watched as Kincaid left the table, then started up the stairs with Rosanna.

"That should take care of him for a while," Will said.

Chapter Seven

Huntsville Unit Penitentiary at Huntsville:

"Twenty years?" the warden said. "Well, Mr. King, it looks like you're gonna be with us for a long, long time. But, if you play by the rules and if you don't make trouble, your stay will be comfortable enough, and who knows, you may get out early. We'll get you assigned to a work detail right away."

When King's in-processing was completed, he was free to step out into the "yard" which was a large open space that was surrounded by a high, fitted-stone wall.

"Well if it ain't Silas King," someone said as soon as King stepped out into the yard.

King was surprised that anyone in here would recognize him and know him well enough to call him Silas. Looking around to see who had addressed him, he saw Kit Chiles.

"What are you doin'?" Chiles asked, and King knew that Chiles was inquiring about the length of his sentence.

"Twenty years," King replied. "You?"

"I'm doin' life."

Shortly after his incarceration, King was forced to shave his beard and cut his hair so that now, the disfigurement of his nose was even more apparent. It wasn't as easy for King, a hierarchy of prisoners had already been established and because he was new, and had a condition of self-importance, he was ostracized or worse.

He was glad that Kit Chiles was also serving time. King and Chiles had actually pulled a few jobs together up around Texarkana, before Chiles was arrested and sent to prison. King had been the boss on those jobs, and Chiles still treated him with deference.

The work details had been the most difficult for Silas, having to put in hours of physical labor when he definitely wasn't in the habit of doing any manual labor at all. One morning, about a week after King arrived, however, the job was no more difficult than mopping the floor in half a dozen rooms. King was in the room where the guards stayed, when he noticed a desk draw was slightly open.

Curiosity overtook him, and looking around to make certain he was alone, King opened the drawer, then gasped in surprise. There were several keys in the drawer and King recognized them as skeleton keys that could possibly fit the locks of every cell. Taking one of the keys, he dropped it into the water of the mop-bucket.

A few minutes later Joshua Simon, the Chief of Guards, came into the room.

"What are you doing in here?" Simon asked, as he moved toward Simon. "No one comes in here except a guard."

"I was told to mop the floors," King responded. "Nobody told me which floors."

That was when Simon noticed that the key drawer was slightly open.

"Drop that mop and hold your hands out," Simon said, as he began a thorough pat down of King.

"What are you looking for, Mr. Simon? Do you think I have a gun?" King asked with a little laugh.

"King, never come into this room again, no matter what anybody tells you," Simon said, when his search produced no results.

"Do you want me to finish the moppin', now that I'm almost done?"

"No, just get out."

"Yes, sir," King said, picking up the bucket.

* * *

Later that night, King hid the key on the windowsill in his cell.

"Chiles," King said the next morning. "If I can find a way to get both of us out of prison, would you be willing to try it?"

"Damn right I'll try it," Chiles said. "When do we do it?"

"I'll let you know. But first we have to do a few things to get ready."

Three nights after getting possession of the key, King lay in his cell, listening to the sound of rattling doors as the night guard came down the corridor checking all the cells. He counted them until he knew the next door the guard would check would be his.

He heard his own door rattle, then the prison guard shined a light into the dark cell until it illuminated the bunk. King was wide awake.

"What you doin' awake, King? I figured for sure you'd be asleep by now," the guard said. "Tomorrow I'll find you somethin' to do like diggin' on the rock pile."

"I can't sleep," King replied.

"Thinking about all your sins, are you?" the guard asked. "I wouldn't be surprised. From what I hear, you've got a lot to atone for."

"I'm just rememberin' how much I enjoyed ever' one

of 'em," King said. "And I'm lookin' forward to gettin' out of here so I can do 'em again."

"Ha!" the guard said. "By the time you get out of here, you'll be way too old for sinnin'."

"How do you know the governor's not goin' to give me a pardon, 'n I'll be out of here before you know it?"

"Governor's pardon. That'll happen when hell freezes over," the guard said, laughing. "I'd better get movin'. Have a good night, King."

"Yeah, you too," King replied.

The guard pulled the light away and once again the cell was plunged into darkness. King lay on his bunk, perfectly still, as he listened to the receding clomp of the guard's footsteps and the echoing rattle of the other cell doors being checked. Counting them, he knew when the last door was checked.

It was a quarter until two in the morning and that meant it would be two hours before the next cell check. Also, the time of two o'clock was important to his escape plan.

When he was certain the guard was gone, he hopped out of bed, then from under his bed, he pulled out an old shirt that he had stolen from the laundry. He had stuffed it with straw he had been secreting out of the stable, so that it formed a ball. Hair and eyebrows, made from real hair, helped create the illusion of a man's face. King put the stuffed ball on the small, thin pillow, then draped the blanket in such a way as to make it appear as if a man was sleeping in the bunk.

That done, King reached up onto the windowsill and found the key he had stolen from the guard room.

Although he had, had the key for a few days, he had never tested it to see if it really worked. He had to choose the right time to make his escape, and tonight was the right time.

King stepped up to the cell door, stuck his arm through the window, inserted the key carefully, then turned and hearing the satisfying click, quietly, pushed the door open. Cautiously, he stuck his head out and looked up and down the long corridor. He saw no one.

King closed the door and locked it behind him, then he looked through the window back into his cell. The dummy was doing its job. From this angle, and in this reduced light, it looked exactly as if he were still in bed.

Quietly, King moved down the corridor then stopped outside one of the cells.

"Chiles?" he whispered in front of one cell. "You ready to go?"

"Son of a bitch, you did it!" Chiles said from the black interior.

"Shh, you got your dummy made?"

"Yeah," Chiles replied.

King opened the door to Chiles' cell, then stepped inside so as not to be seen by any other prisoner who may be awake.

Chiles got his dummy in place, then the two men stepped back out into the corridor. As he had done so with his own cell door, King locked Chiles' door as well so it would withstand the checking of the next, door check.

The two men hurried quickly through the darkness to a barred window at the end of an "L" projection of the corridor. Though the bars on the window looked strong, King knew the window's weakness. While working on a painting detail, he saw that the anchoring bolts were so loose that they could easily be pulled from the wall. That was when King began developing an escape plan and to that end, he painted over the bolts to cover up their weakness.

King pulled on the bars and they came away from the wall, with very little effort. First, he and then Chiles, climbed through the window and dropped onto the ground. Each of them took one of the iron bars to use as a weapon.

Moving swiftly and silently through the dark, they hurried toward the prison dining hall. In just a few minutes, at two o'clock in the morning, a garbage wagon would come from town to haul away all off the prison refuse. There would be two men on the wagon, the driver and the assistant who would be lifting the barrels and dumping the contents into the back of the wagon.

King and Chiles concealed themselves by the area where the dining hall refuse was kept and the smell of it was overpowering.

"I'm goin' to puke if I have to smell this much longer," Chiles complained.

"Go ahead 'n puke if you got to, but be some quiet about it," King said.

King had chosen this night to make his escape, because this was the night the garbage would be picked up and it was the first quarter of the moon.

"Shuck out of your clothes," King said.

"Oh, no, I ain't gonna stand here naked."

"Do it. We don't have much time."

They heard the sound off the approaching wagon and they gripped their weapons.

"You goin' to have to help me with this'n Arnie, they's always more here 'n just about anywhere else," the assistant driver said as the wagon came to a stop.

"Now, Gus, don't I always, hep ya?" Arnie replied as he set the brake, tied off the reins and jumped down to help.

King and Chiles watched until the last can was emptied into the wagon, then with a nod from King, they stepped out in front of the two men.

"What the hell! You ain't supposed to be here?" Arnie

said, but before he, or Gus could call out, King and Chiles brought the iron bars down on their heads. The two men went down.

"Get their clothes 'n their hats," King ordered.

"Damn, these here clothes stink,"

"You want to try 'n drive through the gate naked?"

Quickly, King and Chiles stripped the clothes off the unconscious Arnie and Gus, and then put their clothes on as fast as possible.

"Climb up there," King said as he scrambled up, released the brake, and started toward the gate.

"Hey, how come you reckon their ain't been no alarm bells or nothin'?" Chiles asked.

"Now, why do you think the reason is, that we ain't heard no alarms?" King asked.

"The dummies?"

"Yeah, I doubt they'll even know we're gone 'till mornin'."

As they passed the kennel, the dogs started barking.

"What's got the dogs all upset, do you suppose?" one of the gate guards asked.

"More'n likely, it's the garbage wagon comin' back," the other guard answered. "They smell all that food 'n think it's the finest feast in Huntsville."

The first guard laughed. "Hell, none o' this shit is

worth eatin' even before it becomes garbage."

Both men laughed.

"Listen, let's get the gate open now, so's they can drive right on through. Ain't no need of havin' to smell that wagon any longer 'n we got to."

The guard nodded at someone who was up on the wall and the gate, assisted by swinging weights, opened-up, just as King and Chiles drove through, unchallenged.

"How long you think it'll be before them two fellers come to?" Chiles asked.

"I expect it won't be long now, but even when they do wake up, they're goin' to be some addled, 'n more 'n likely won't even remember what happened to 'em. But, at any rate, we need to get shed of this wagon, soon as we're far enough away so's the tower guards can't see us."

This, King knew, was the most dangerous part of the entire plan. Once Arnie and Gus came too, everyone would know that some prisoners had escaped on the garbage wagon and a garbage wagon would be easily seen by the tower guards. They were helped by the fact that it was dark and though the mirror backed lanterns could throw the powerful light beams quite a long way from the walls, as soon as they were beyond the range of the search lights, they could abandon the wagon.

"Now," King said.

"You goin' to stop the wagon, or what?" Chiles asked.

"No, if we just jump down the mules will, more 'n likely keep goin', 'n that might lead 'em away from us."

Both King and Chiles dropped to the ground and let the wagon continue on its way.

"What do we do now?" Chiles asked.

"We need to get as far away from the prison as we can," King replied, "cause they'll be turning out the dogs." Walking and even running some, and going through any little creek they could find, they continued their getaway until sunrise. From the top of a hill, they saw a small building with a small curl of smoke coming from the chimney. The smell of cooking bacon was in the air.

"Mr. Chiles, if I invited you to eat breakfast with me, would you do it?"

"Damn right I would," Chiles responded, going along with the little joke.

Half-an-hour later, a man came out of the little house, still eating a biscuit. King watched as the he saddled his horse, then rode off to tend to the day's chores.

Slowly, King and Chiles moved down the hill to the shack, then King sneaked up to look through the window. As he had hoped, and expected, it was empty.

King turned to wave a signal to Chiles, who moved quickly across the open area to join King.

"It's empty," he said. "And my invitation to breakfast still stands."

Inside proved to be a bonanza for the two men. They made a meal of biscuits and bacon. They also found a shirt for each of them, but the real prize was a pistol belt, complete with a .44 Colt, a double barreled .12 gauge shotgun and fourteen dollars and twenty five cents in an empty coffee can.

Chapter Eight

From the Toyah Weekly Defender:

PRISON ESCAPE

Silas King and Kit Chiles the escapees. Residents of Toyah will remember that it was but a few weeks previous when King was tried in the local courthouse, found guilty of attempted kidnapping, and accessory to murder of Arthur Sinclair. Because none of the bullets in Sinclair's body matched the caliber of his pistol, King was not found guilty of murder.

If seen, citizens are cautioned not to attempt to apprehend Silas King, or his fellow escapee, themselves.

"The son of a bitch escaped," Gid said handing the paper he had just read to Will.

"Well, I don't expect he'll be our problem. He would have to be really dumb to come around here."

"What are you talking about, Big Brother? He *is* that dumb," Gid said.

Will chuckled. "You know what? I wouldn't put it past him if he came right back to Toyah."

Committing two low level robberies of unprotected country stores and killing three people, provided Silas King and Kit Chiles with a little over four hundred dollars. Four hundred dollars was a year's salary for a cowboy and it was enough money to allow King and Chiles to come by some necessities, such as another pistol, two rifles and a change of clothes.

Now King and Chiles were visiting with Sly Aikens at a table in a run-down saloon. King and Aikens had been part of another gang, long ago.

"Sly, this here's Kit Chiles. Me 'n him was together for a while," King said.

Aikens laughed. "Yeah, I know where you two was together at. It was in all the papers. I'll tell you this, that was some slick escape."

"Hush up, you damn fool," King warned.

"Oh, sorry," Aikens said.

"We need to put us together a gang agin," King said. "When I was sent up, my buddies sort of spread out all over." King didn't say that everyone had been killed. "Do you think you can come up with a couple good men? You,

77

too, Chiles. You know anybody hangin' around?"

"I can get Val Baker," Aikens said. "He got out of prison about a year ago. Last I seen him, he was trying to make it as a sodbuster, but it ain't workin' out so good for him."

"And I know a guy name of Perry Hoy," Chiles said.

"That's a start, but we'll need more . . . wait a minute," King said. He signaled one of the bar girls, and with an expectant smile, she came over to the table.

"You looking for some company, honey?" she asked.

"No, we've got business to discuss, but do you see that man standing there at the end of the bar? I'll give you a dollar if you'll bring him over here."

"A dollar?" the girl smiled. "I'd have to sell twenty drinks to get a dollar. All right, honey, I'll get him for you."

A moment later the bar girl returned with the man who had been at the end of the bar. He was clean shaven and was good enough looking that he had already attracted the attention of all the bar girls in the saloon. It was only his lack of funds that kept him from accepting any of the solicitations.

The young man approached the table with a confused expression on his face.

"Did you want to see me?" he asked.

"Your name's Fred Bell ain't it?" King asked with a welcoming smile.

78

"Silas King," Bell said with a smile as genuine as King's. "Why, I haven't seen you since . . ."

"The battle at Shawneetown, Kansas," King said. "Join us."

"I don't know about that. I think I saw your name in the paper here recently," Bell said.

"You plannin' on turning me in, Bell?" King asked, with an edge to his words.

Bell smiled. "The way I see it, whatever a man does is his own business. Anyway, I'd never turn against someone I rode during the war. We all got troubles enough."

"How much money do you have?" King asked.

"Not much, but I'd lend you half of what I got if you need something to tide you over until you get on your feet," Bell said. "I been aiming to put together enough money to get me to California, but work is slow around here."

King laughed out loud. "Do you see what I mean, fellers, about old pards? Here, Fred ain't seen me in who knows how long, but he's willin' to lend me some money if I need it."

King turned to Fred.

"Listen, I don't want any of your money. Truth is, I'm about to give you a chance to make some money. A lot of money."

"What is it I have to do?" Fred asked.

"Nothin' no more 'n we used to do durin' the war. I'm puttin' some men together, 'n I figure we can hit a few stagecoaches 'n maybe a train or two and pretty soon we'll be making some real money. What do you say?"

"I don't know," Fred said. "I haven't done anything like that since the war, but like I said, I'd like to get to California. I want to open a furniture building shop there."

"Hell, you can prob'ly make that much money on our first job," King said. He smiled again. "Soon as I get enough of a gang together, I aim to rob me a train. Are you in?"

"Silas, I want to say no, but I've been hanging around this town for several months, now, and I'm not any closer to California than I was when I got here. Would you take me if I said I only wanted to be in on one job?"

King smiled. "I'll take you cause I need men—men I can trust, but I've got me an idea that as soon as you find out how much money you can make, why, you'll stay with me."

"We'll see," Fred said.

Long Trail Ranch:

Julia was sound asleep when she heard a pecking sound on her window.

Peck. A few seconds, then another peck. A few seconds

then another peck and curious as to what it might be, she got out of bed to investigate. When she looked down into the darkness, she saw Jamie Kincaid. He had a few more pebbles in his hand, so she knew he was the one who had been trying to get her attention. With a broad smile, Kincaid gave a big wave to Julia.

The morning sun splashed golden bars of light through the kitchen window. Frying bacon was twitching in the pan and it and the smell of coffee, added to the welcoming aroma.

"Maria, are the biscuits ready?" Ethyl Abernathy asked.

"Si, Senora."

Ethyl smiled. "Then I would say it's about time to call everyone to breakfast, wouldn't you?"

"I will put the biscuits on the table," Maria replied.

"John? Julia? Breakfast is ready!" Ethyl called.

John arrived almost as soon as he was called.

"You don't have to call me twice," John said. "Biscuits, bacon, eggs, flapjacks, coffee, now I would say this is a meal fit for a king."

Maria laughed. "Maybe for a *Jefe*, no?"

"Julia?" Ethyl called again. "Julia, honey, it's time for breakfast. You need to get ready for school."

Again, she got no answer.

"What in the world is wrong with that girl?" Ethyl asked.

"She's normally as quick to respond to breakfast as you are. I'd better go wake her up or she'll hold up the wagon."

As Ethel started up the stairs, John picked up a biscuit and took a bite.

"Uh, uhm" John said. "Maria, you make the best biscuits in the world."

Maria smiled, and with a slight blush replied. "Oh, Senor, I think you just like biscuits."

Before John could reply, he heard a blood curdling scream from the second floor. Dropping his biscuit on the table, John ran toward the sound of the scream, taking the stairs two at a time.

"Ethyl! What is it? What' wrong?"

With his heart beating rapidly in fear, John hurried to Julia's room where he saw Ethyl standing there with tears streaming down her face. She was holding a note, which she handed to John.

Mama, Papa

Jamie has come to get me. I love him very much and we want to be married soon. I want to be with him. Please do not try and stop me. I will write to you when we are settled.

Love

Julia

"Oh, John, we can't let her do this," Ethyl said. "Jamie Kincaid. Can't she see what an evil man he is? You have to do whatever it takes to bring her back!"

* * *

Will and Gid were in the Neighborhood Cafe having coffee with Mike Blanton, editor and publisher of the *Toyah Weekly Defender*.

"I have to give Silas King and Kit Chiles credit for arranging a pretty daring escape," Blanton said. "Knocking out the garbage men and then stealing the wagon is a pretty good plan."

"Does anybody know how the two men are doing? They didn't die, did they?" Will asked.

"The last I heard, they came through with no problems," Jensen said. "With what we know about King, it's a wonder he didn't kill 'em."

"That's your headline for the next newspaper," Gid said. "Garbage men survive brutal attack. Use the word brutal. That's what folks like to read."

"I haven't chosen the headline yet. Since King was captured and tried here, we have a little more proprietary interest than most other newspapers."

"We should have killed the son of a bitch when we had the chance," Gid said.

"We should have killed him way back in Lawrence," Will said. "We saw what he did to those people and if he was dead, I'll bet at least two dozen people would still be alive."

"I'd say more than that," Gid said, "especially if you count the men, he hoodwinked into riding with him."

"Do either of you know anything about the man who escaped with him?" Blanton asked.

"Kit Chiles," Will said. "Yeah, we know him. He was another one of Quantrill's raiders. I can't say that we rode with him very often, the same with King. It's one thing to blow up railroads and interrupt supply lines going to the Union Army, but when you have a bunch of men who were motivated by the pure joy of killing, then that's something else."

"With the two of us, what we did was for revenge," Gid said. "I'll never get over what the damn Yankees did to our mom and dad."

"If it weren't for the Yankees, you'd be back in Missouri walking behind a mule. A whole passel of kids would be trailin' along behind," Will said.

Gid got a wistful expression on his face. "And sometimes I think that wouldn't be a bad life."

"You mean you don't want to settle in Toyah permanently?" Blanton asked. "I think this town has sort of gotten used to you two. You could do worse than settle here."

"Now what would we do to make a living?" Will said. "You've been in a couple of poker games with my brother, and it hasn't been too pretty."

Blanton laughed. "I guess you could say the newspaper didn't need as much advertising this issue, thanks to Gid."

"I still think you cheated," Gid said.

"Isn't that Colonel Abernathy?" Blanton said, as he pointed to a man across the street. "It's rather unusual to see him in town at this time of day, especially going into the saloon."

"He probably heard that King escaped, and he's worried about it," Gid said. "But who can blame him?"

Abernathy left the saloon after only a few minutes and crossed the street to the café. When he stepped in, he saw Will and Gid and started toward them. The fact that he didn't smile upon seeing them, but had instead, a very concerned expression, tended to validate Gid's observation.

"Colonel, pull up a chair and join us," Will invited. "You look like a man on a mission."

"Boys, I have to talk to you."

The tone of John's voice, and the expression on his face told Will that, whatever it was, it was very serious.

"I, uh," John looked at the newspaper editor. "Mike, if

you don't mind, could you excuse us for a few minutes?"

"Certainly," Blanton said. "But you know that it's the curse of the newspaper man always to be curious. I need to get back to my office anyway, so I'll not interfere with your meeting. But, if it develops into news, you'll let me know, won't you?"

"Thank you," John replied without giving the newspaper editor a direct answer.

"Now, Colonel, sit down and tell us what's on your mind," Will invited.

John took the proffered chair, but he said nothing. He pinched the bridge of his nose, and squeezed his eyes shut. Then, after a long moment of silence, he spoke. "She's gone," he said, breaking on the words, but by a supreme effort, managing to keep from crying.

"Who's gone?"

"Julia," John said, barely able to choke the word out. He paused for a moment, took several deep breaths, then continued. "This morning, when we called her to breakfast, she didn't come down. Her mother went up to check on her, and this is what she found."

John showed Will and Gid the note Julia had written.

"All I ask is that you find her, boys. Please find her." This time, John couldn't hold back the tears.

Will and Gid thought the best place to start would be with

the Long Trail ranch hands. They concentrated primarily on Tater Wyatt, Gabby Harris, Eddie Malloy and Harry Slater, the men who had shared the bunkhouse with Jamie Kincaid. Leo Hunter was present as well.

"I never liked that son of a bitch no how," Malloy said.

"Kincaid talked about El Paso all the time," Gabby Harris said.

"Yeah," Slater said. "He used to live there and sometimes when he'd get pissed off about something, he said he was goin' back. So, if you was to ask me, if he really did take Miss Abernathy with him, why, more 'n likely he took her to El Paso."

"Yeah," Leo said. "I'd say El Paso would be a good bet. The dumb son of a bitch probably thinks if he can get Julia that far away from home, nobody will be able to find them. Maybe he even thinks he can sneak her over the border and hide out for as long as it takes."

"Thanks, men," Will said. "You've been a big help."

When Will told John the general consensus of the men, it was decided that the Crocketts would head for El Paso. All three were aware that it was a long shot that Jamie and Julia would be there, but with no better lead, they had to start somewhere.

"Take the train to El Paso," John said. "I'll have a stock car put on for your horses, so that once you get there, you can start your search immediately."

"I know it's hard, Colonel, but try not to worry about Julia. You know what a spunky girl she is. I have a feeling she'll be all right," Gid said.

"I hope you're right, but she's just a sixteen-year-old child. And Kincaid, I saw how he was making Julia feel." John buried his face in his hands. "This is all my fault. I should have fired him months ago."

"We'll find her," Will said. "No matter where it takes us, we'll find her,"

In Will's mind, he wasn't sure. In most cases, when he and Gid were hired to go after people, they were looking for people who didn't want to be taken. In this case, if he had read Julia's note correctly, she wasn't in anyway forced to leave. This could take a long time, but they would find Julia wherever she was.

Texas and Pacific Railroad Depot - Toyah

Will and Gid were loading Pepper and Scout onto the stock car that had been attached to the first train going west.

"Here are your tickets," John said as he walked toward the chartered car. "And here's five hundred dollars for your expenses. It's on top of the money you'll get when you bring Julia back to me."

"Thanks, Colonel. That's very generous of you."

"I'm telling you again. It doesn't matter what I have to do or pay to get my daughter back. Do you understand what I'm saying?"

"Yes, sir," Gid said, "and we'll do our best to get her home as soon as possible."

The train whistle blew, and the conductor called out.

"All aboard!"

John extended his hand to Will and then Gid, but no one said a word.

Chapter Nine

Eagle Spring Way Station:

Eagle Spring Way Station was forty miles southwest of Toyah, and about ten miles beyond the town of Jericho. The Way Station wasn't a depot as such, because there was no provision for buying tickets, though from time to time people could board the train and made arrangements with the conductor for passage to the next destination.

Eagle Spring served two purposes for the railroad, and it was for those reasons that the Texas and Pacific Railroad had built and staffed the way station.

The primary purpose was to provide a watering stop for the four trains that came through daily. The northeast bound trains were scheduled at eight in the morning, and two in the afternoon, and the southwest bound trains at ten in the morning, and four in the afternoon, but seldom were they on time.

The way station, which also served as a telegraph station, was manned by Boston "Buck" Godfrey and his daughter, Leah. Because of the tendency for the trains to perpetually run behind schedule, it was necessary to transmit, as much as possible, the exact location of the train traffic. As the two o'clock northeast bound train had already passed, the Godfreys were preparing for the southwest bound train.

The Texas and Pacific Railroad allowed Buck to run a small store out of the way station. It served as a convenience for ranchers and farmers who were able to take advantage of the service between shopping excursions to one of the bigger towns, like Jericho, or Terlingua, Texas.

Leah, an exceptionally pretty young woman, was bent over a washboard when the telegraph began to clatter.

"Papa?" she called.

"I've got it, darlin'," Buck said hurrying to the instrument. He responded with his acknowledgement and the telegraph began to send a message.

Buck recorded the message as he received it, then keyed in his response, the key grew quiet.

"Well, what do you know?" he said.

"What is it, Papa?"

"The west bound has a clear track to Salcedo. It's also carrying quite a bit of money on this trip."

"Did they say how much?"

"Not in so many words, but if I understand the code, I'd say the amount would be close to fifty thousand dollars," Buck said. "Don't you know some outlaw would like to know that? I wonder how much we could get, if we sold that information?"

"Papa!" Leah said loudly. "Don't even think those words!"

Buck laughed. "You're right. If we did do that, maybe we could have adjoining rooms in Huntsville Prison."

"You, not me," Leah said. "I'd turn you in before you could say Jack Robinson."

"You would do that, wouldn't you," Buck said as he started toward the water tank. "I'd better make sure the tank's full and the spout's clear."

"And I'd better get the clothes hung out to dry," Leah said as she returned to her task.

Terlingua, Texas

Silas King's newly formed gang consisted of Kit Chiles, who was second only to Silas King in authority. In addition, there were Perry Hoy, Val Baker, Abe Haller, Sly Aikens, and Fred Bell.

"Fifty thousand dollars," King said. "That train's carrying fifty thousand dollars."

"Whoee!" Haller said. "How do you know it's a' carryin' that much money?"

"A couple of gold pieces and the telegraph feller here, told me."

"And how much does he get for tellin' us that?" Chiles asked.

"He thinks he's gettin' five hunnert dollars," King said with a smile. "But I ain't plannin' on givin' him nothin' more'n he already got."

"Fifty thousand dollars!" Sly Aikens said. "Damn, that's purt' nigh all the money they is in the world."

"Uh, uh, no it ain't," Baker said. "They tells it Vanderbilt's got more 'n a million dollars his ownself."

"It don't matter none," Hoy said. "Fifty thousand dollars is a lot o' money 'n I'd love to get my hands on it."

"We will, if ever' body does what I tell 'em to do," King said. He looked directly at Fred Bell. "Do ya think you can handle getting' so much money, Bell?"

"If you think we can do it, I'm in, but don't you think they'll be an armed guard for that kind of money?"

"Don't matter. We can take 'em out. They think they're movin' this kinda money on the quiet," King said, "but they ain't a doin' it."

Two hours later, King and his men were waiting in a copse of trees, less than half a mile from the way station at Eagle Spring.

"We'll hear the train whistling to let the station man know that it's comin' in for water, 'n when it stops all we have to do is ask for the money and they'll give it up without 'ny problem at all."

"How do we know it will be all that easy?" Haller asked.

King grinned. "Cause we'll kill the engineer and the fireman if they don't turn the money over to us."

"King, you aren't planning on really killing anyone, are you?" Fred Bell said.

"I'm plannin' on makin' 'em think I am," King replied, "but if it takes, pullin' the trigger, I'll sure as hell do it. I ain't lettin' that money get away, and with seven of us, you know we got more'n they'll have guardin' the box."

"Look, Silas, I didn't come with you to be a part of killing engineers and firemen. I think when this is over, I'll just mosey on my way," Fred Bell said.

"But you'll not turn down your share of the money, huh," Chiles said. "I don't think that's the way it works in this gang."

"Lay off him, Kit," King said. "If he don't want no part of this, let the son of a bitch go on his way. But I'm bettin' he can't turn his back on us, when he sees what his take's gonna be."

"I don't need that much money," Fred said. "You can

keep my share. All I need is enough to let me get to California 'n open up a furniture makin' shop."

"That's fair," King said, "but I'm gonna be askin' ya agin' when we ride out of here with our saddlebag's full of money."

Julia and Jamie Kincaid had been on the road for a week, camping out at night. Kincaid hadn't come to her since they left the ranch and, the first night she was surprised and a little disappointed that he hadn't even kissed her. But, as she thought about it, she realized that this wasn't the way she wanted it to be anyway. She would want them to be married and she decided she respected Jamie for waiting.

However, and this she thought was strange, Jamie not only did not share her blanket at night, it seemed to her that he was growing more distant. She didn't understand why that would be. Certainly, they could be affectionate with one another, without violating her innocence.

On this, their seventh day since leaving the ranch, they left any semblance of following the main road and now they seemed to be finding trails that were little more than paths. At first, she had thought that they were doing this to avoid being followed and it made sense to her. Julia was certain that as soon as her father discovered her note, he would either look for her himself, or else hire someone to come after her. She thought his first choice would probably be Will and Gid Crockett, the same men he had hired to accompany her to her aunt's house. But now she had no idea where they were going and for the whole week, they had never once gone near a town, a settlement, or even a ranch house. She was beginning to question her choice of leaving home.

"I love you, Jamie," she said, when the trail was wide enough for two horses to be side by side.

He didn't answer. He didn't even look at her. As she thought about it, she realized that not since that first night when he had coaxed her to leave with him, had he told her that he loved her.

"Where are we going?" Julia asked.

"We'll be there soon," Kincaid replied.

"I think I will like El Paso."

"What makes you think that's where we are going?"

"Because you always talked about how beautiful it is. I just thought that was where we would be going."

"Don't you think that's where they'd look for us first?" Kincaid asked.

Julia shrugged her shoulders. "I want to know, why haven't you told me you love me? You do love me, don't you?"

"How old are you?"

"You know how old I am. I'm sixteen."

"That's right. Now tell me, don't you think a man wants a woman that knows how to treat a man. A more experienced woman?"

"I . . . I suppose so," Julia said. "It's just that, when we were together, you never said anything like this. If you don't want me, why did you come and get me?"

"Grow up," Kincaid replied, harshly. "Try and not be a foolish little girl all the time."

"Jamie . . . don't you . . ." but she didn't finish the question, because she feared the answer.

"Don't I what?" Jamie asked.

Julia was going to asked him again if he loved her, but this wasn't the man she had known. What happened to the Jamie who she used to sit by on the wagon trips to and from school? He used to tease her and go out of his way to do things for her. What happened to that Jamie?

"Jamie?" she said tentatively.

"What now?"

"I've changed my mind. I want to go home." Tears filled her eyes.

"You'll go home when your Papa pays for you."

"What?" Julia gasped. "Jamie, what does that mean?"

"Come on, you're a smart girl. You figure it out."

Kincaid took his lariat, opened up a loop and dropped it around Julia, then tightened it.

"Now that you know what the game is, I don't want

you to get it in your head that you can head on back to your papa, that is if he would even take you now."

Julia started to answer, but then she didn't say anything. What if Jamie was right? What if her father didn't care that she had run away? What if he didn't send someone to look for her?

For the rest of the afternoon, they continued the slow progress, marked only by the footfalls of the horses.

Julia continued to weep, though now her sobs were silent.

What had she done?

Chapter Ten

From where seven men were waiting, they heard the distant sound of a train whistle.

"All right boys," King said, raising his hand, "if we move now, we'll get there just about the time the train stops. They won't be expectin' nothin' like us showin' up, so they won't be anyways they can put up a fight."

"That fifty thousand dollars is our'n," Haller yelled. "I can smell it now. All's I need is to touch it in my hand." He spurred his horse and started out at a gallop.

"Hold up, there," Chiles yelled. "You want to get us all kilt? We'll do this together, just the way Silas says."

On board the train

Will Crockett had been counting the time between the mile markers. "Thirty miles to the hour," he announced.

"Don't you have anything better to do than to count the mile-markers?" Gid asked.

"We're on a train, Gid. What do you suggest I do?"

"I don't know. Look out the window, maybe?"

Will chuckled. "I'm counting mile markers, they're outside the train, which means I am looking through the window."

"I guess you are," Gid conceded. I wonder how much longer before we get to El Paso."

"We've got a little while to go yet," Will said. "But I think we should be there before dark."

"First thing I want to do is find someplace to have supper," Gid said. "They'll be some little old lady who makes the best tamales in the whole state of Texas. She'll have a little stand, and I'll buy everyone she's got left."

"I have no doubt that you could do that."

The train began to slow, noticeably, and as the conductor was passing down the aisle at that moment, Will questioned him.

"Where are we, Mr. Gillespie? Why are we stopping?"

"This is Eagle Spring, and we'll be taking on water here," Gillespie said.

"Eagle Spring? Is that a new town that has sprung up?"

"No, just a way station, but it's a little more than that. The telegraph operator runs a little general store, so it's more than the normal way station. Sometimes when this run is late, the girl puts out some fresh bread and butter. Tastes real good."

"Do people get off the train?" Gid asked.

"Sure. We'll be here at least a half hour, sometimes longer."

"Then I say, we see if she's got any bread," Gid said.

"Before, we do that," Will said, "why don't we let Pepper and Scout out for a little water and exercise. You know damn well they're nervous about being cooped up in that stock car."

"Yeah, sounds like a good idea," Gid agreed. "I'll find a watering trough while you stay with the horses."

"You mean so you can scope out the food, don't you? We'll both tend to the horses, and then we'll see if there's time to eat a bite."

As soon as the train stopped, the two brothers stepped down from the passenger car, then walked back to the stock car, pulled the sliding ramp down, then climbed up to open the door.

As Will and Gid led the horses down the ramp, a very pretty young woman came toward them from the building.

"Oh, those are beautiful horses," she said with a broad smile.

"Why, thank you, ma'am," Gid said. "Did I miss you on the train?"

The girl laughed. "No, no, I live here."

"Here?" Gid asked, surprised by the information. "Then you're the bread lady."

"Some people call me that, but my name is Leah Godfrey. This is Eagle Spring Way Station, and Buck, that is, my father, and I run it."

"It must get awfully lonely for you living out here in such an isolated place," Will said.

"Not really. If all goes well, four trains come through every day, and almost always someone will get off for a few minutes. And the farmers and ranchers in the area, will sometimes come to the store to buy something to hold them over until they can get into town. But you are right to one degree. It isn't possible to actually make friends under such conditions."

"Well, how about we be friends?" Gid suggested.

Leah's smile broadened. "Yes, I think I could accept that. What are your names?"

"I'm Gid Crockett, and my big brother here is Will."

"Big brother?" Leah asked, surprised by the comment as, examining the two men it was odd that Gid, who was over six feet tall and about two-hundred pounds of muscle, would refer to Will, who was about five eight, and considerably slighter of build, as his big brother.

"He's always been my big brother, because he's always older than I am."

Again, Leah laughed. "I suppose I can understand if . . ."

Whatever Leah was going to say was interrupted by gunfire as seven men came riding up through a draw with guns blazing.

Shooting off the guns had the effect of keeping everyone else on the train.

"Leah," Will hissed. "Get down behind that boulder."

Leah did as she was ordered.

"Gid, you get behind that rock, and get down in this ditch," Will ordered.

"You in the mail car," one of the outlaws called out. "We know you're a carryin' a strong box, so throw it down now, 'fore we start killin'. We're a startin' with the engineer, and then the fireman, and then we'll be startin' on anybody else who's on this galloper."

Will fired a shot into the air, getting their immediate attention. "Drop your guns."

A couple of the outlaws shot at Will, but the bullets hit the rocks, then whined off into empty space.

"Kill 'em!" one of the outlaws shouted, and they started shooting at Will.

Then both brothers returned fire, and immediately, three of the outlaws went down. "Get the hell out of here!" one of the outlaws shouted, and the four remaining outlaws abandoned the field.

Will and Gid threw a few more shots at the retreating riders but they were designed more to run them off, than to kill any of them.

"Leah, were you hit?" Will asked as he moved toward the girl who was still hiding behind the biggest boulder.

"I'm fine, but I must find Papa," Leah shouted in concern as she hurried toward the way stop building. She didn't get a quarter of the way before a tall, slender man with a well-developed handlebar moustache came out of the office, running toward Leah. The two met and embraced in the middle.

"Was anyone hurt on the train or in the way station?" Will asked when he reached the two.

"We're the only two here, and I don't think anyone had time to get off the train," Buck replied. "I'm just thankful that you two were where you were when this happened."

Gid had gone to check on the downed men, his gun still drawn. He found two of the three outlaws were obviously dead, but the third one groaned.

"This one's alive, Will."

The masked outlaw opened his eyes and looked at the two men who were leaning over him.

"The Crocketts?" the outlaw questioned, calmly.

"What the hell?" Gid said as he reached down to yank the injured man's mask away.

"I'll be damn," Will said. "Fred Bell! Didn't we just have a drink with you in some Podunk town—what, six months ago? What in the hell are you doing here?"

"It looks like I was trying to rob a train," Bell said with a little self-deprecating chuckle. "But I don't think I did that good of a job of it."

"Are you hurt?" Will asked.

"I think so." He put his hand to his side, and it was soon dripping with blood.

"Do you think you can ride?" Gid asked.

"I guess I'm going to have to. Unless you want to leave me out here for the coyotes," Fred said.

"Get him into the way station. I'll take a look at him," Leah said.

"You?" Gid asked.

"I've learned some nursing, along the way," Leah said. "As isolated as we are, it's come in handy."

The train was still sitting there and the conductor came up to talk to Will and Gid.

"Mister Crockett we've only got a few minutes left before we have to clear the track, so if you're going to put your horses back on the car, you'd better do it now."

"We'll be staying," Will said. "But if you would, would you take—" Will halted in mid-sentence. "Fred, I suppose you know these men; what are their names?"

"That would be Sly Aikens," Bell said, pointing to one of the men, "And that one would be Abe Haller."

Will nodded, then turned back to the conductor. "I'd be obliged if you'd record their names and then load the bodies on the train, maybe in the stock car. You can drop them off at the next town. I just don't want to have to bury them here."

Gillespie nodded. "I'll get a couple of men to help me get 'em on board."

"Fred, wait here for a moment while Gid and I get our saddles and tack."

"I don't reckon I'll be goin' anywhere," Fred replied.

With their tack retrieved, they returned to the, still-living outlaw. "Fred, do you think you can walk over to the building, or should I try to find you and your friends horses?"

"Don't call them my friends. Look where it got me."

With Gid on one side, and Will on the other, they walked toward the low lying, but spread out building that was the way station.

By the time they reached the building, they heard the short blast of the whistle and looking back, saw the engineer waving at them. After that, there was a loud, large puff of steam, then the clanking of the couplers taking up slack as the train began rolling. It gained momentum quickly, and within a short time was speeding away from them.

"Take him in there," Leah ordered, once they were inside. She pointed to a small room off the large central area. "There's a bed in there."

"Ma'am, if you put me in there, I'll bleed all over your

bed sheet," Fred said.

"Rather the bed than the floor," Leah replied. "It's easier to wash the bed sheets than it is to scrub the floor."

They lay their patient on the bed, then Leah began cutting away his shirt.

"Are you sure you have to cut it off, ma'am?" Bell asked. "This is my only shirt."

"This is a general store; we have more shirts."

"What happened to you, Fred?"

"What do you mean what happened to me? I got shot," Fred replied. "You ought to know that, seeing as you're the ones that shot me.

"No, I mean, how did you wind up trying to rob a train? Last time we saw you, you said you were on your way to California."

"I figured I needed a little traveling money," Fred said.

"You folks know each other?" Buck Godfrey asked, surprised by the dialogue between the two men.

"Let's just say that we rode together during the war," Will said, without being any more specific.

"It doesn't look all that bad," Leah reported, after examining her patient. "The bullet hit on the extreme outside and sort of cut a little ridge on through. Actually, it looks like it's pretty superficial. I can clean it up, pour on a little alcohol, put on a bandage, and he'll be good to go."

"Good to go?" Fred asked. "Go where? Miss, are you

telling me I haven't made a very good first impression with you?" he teased.

Despite the situation, Leah laughed. "Well, you did try and rob the train, and you got yourself shot in the process. What do you think?"

"Well, yeah, I mean, if you want to put it that way," Fred replied with a little laugh.

"Fred, did I see Silas King with you?" Will asked.

"That's entirely possible, because he was with us."

"I have to say that I was surprised to see him. If he had any sense, after escaping from prison, he would be long gone from here."

"You remember King, Will. His mind doesn't work like everybody else's."

All the time they were talking, Leah was busy treating Fred. When his wound was cleaned, and he had on a different shirt, Will and Gid began to discuss what they should do with him.

"But what about Julia," Gid said. "Have you forgotten why we were on this train?"

"I know, but a little something has come up."

"Who is Julia?" Leah asked.

"It's a long story," Will said, but he carefully explained the situation as well as he could. He thought maybe a woman would have a different perspective.

"If they are in love, why would her father interfere?"

Leah asked.

"The girl is sixteen, and the daughter of a very wealthy man. The man worked on the ranch as a cow hand, and not that that is a bad thing, but he is thirty-two years old." Gid said.

"Oh," Leah replied. "Oh, my. It would seem that if the man was an acceptable husband, the two would have stayed with the blessings of the father. I can see the girl's running away would be a cause for concern."

"I don't think concern is a strong enough word," Will said. "They were caught in—shall we say a compromising position, and I do believe if Gid and I had not been there, Jamie Kincaid would be dead."

"All right, then I can say we're going on to El Paso to look for Julia. But what are we going to do about Fred?" Gid asked.

"We can't leave him here, and he can't go with us, so there's only one thing we can do," Will said. "We're going to have to take him back to Jericho and turn him over to the sheriff."

"Do you think you can ride, Fred?" Gid asked.

"Yeah, it's not a ride I want to take, but I'm up to it."

"We'll do what we can for you," Will said. "Nobody was killed, and no money was taken."

"Seeing as how this was the first thing I ever did, that is since the war ended, I hope the judge will take that into consideration and be lenient with me."

"Well, maybe they won't do too much to you," Gid said, "but it's probably a good idea to clear your name. Everybody who rode for Quantrill knows what it's like to always be looking over your shoulder, waiting for some bounty hunter to shoot you in the back."

A few minutes later, as Will and Gid were getting ready to go, Leah came to speak privately to them.

"Where will you be taking him?" she asked.

"I expect we'll be taking him to the sheriff in Jericho, whoever that is," Will replied.

"That would be Patrick O'Shea," Leah said. "Do you have to take him there?"

"Where else would we take him? That's the closest town isn't it?"

"I mean, do you have to take him at all?"

"Is Sheriff O'Shea a fair man?" Will asked.

"Yes, I think he is."

"Then that's the best that Fred can hope for. If this really was his first holdup, it means he doesn't have a record. With a fair trial, I doubt that he would get more than a year in prison, if that much."

"I hope not," Leah said. "He seems like such a nice young man. I know, he tried to rob the train, but nothing happened, I mean they didn't even get any of the money."

"When they hold his trial, we'll testify for him," Will promised.

Chapter Eleven

"Fred, there are three horses outside. Which one is yours?" Will asked, as he and Gid were preparing to take him into town.

"The one with a white stocking left forefoot."

"I'll take the saddles off the other two, and put 'em in the corral," Buck Godfrey said. "I don't expect anybody'd come claim 'em, but you tell the sheriff we got 'em."

"I'll let Sheriff O'Shea know they're here," Will said.

Fred was able to walk on his own, though Leah walked beside him to steady him as they came outside.

"How long of a ride is it to Jericho?" Gid asked.

"It's about two hours," Buck said. "You can't get lost, just follow Squaw Creek."

"Squaw Creek, not the railroad tracks?" Gid replied.

"By Squaw Creek, it's no more 'n ten miles," Buck said. "Fifteen by the tracks."

"All right, Squaw Creek it is."

"Do you need help getting mounted?" Will asked.

"No, I can do it," Fred replied, even as he was swinging into the saddle.

"Thanks for the help," Will said to Buck and Leah as the three of them rode off.

"Fred, you aren't going to try to run away, are you?" Gid asked.

"Nope. I'm good," Fred replied.

"Are you sure this train robbery was the first thing you ever tried to pull with this gang?" Will asked, as the three men rode together on the way to Jericho.

"Yeah, like I told you before, I was just going to put together enough money to get me to California. I even told them they could keep my share of the fifty thousand dollars that they were going to get from the train robbery."

"Fifty thousand dollars? Where'd you get a crazy figure like that?" Will asked.

"That's what Silas told us. Said he had bribed a tele-graph operator to get the information."

Will chuckled. "I can't believe King got bamboozled by a flimflam man. There wasn't any money on that train, at least not that kind of money. Did you see a single guard, anywhere, Gid?"

"Not that I saw," Gid said. "If we hadn't been where we were to run King and his men off, and they would have really shot the engineer like they were threatening, you'd be in a heap more trouble than you are right now, Fred."

"I know. I've been thinking about that."

"Do you have any paper out on you?" Will asked.

"I don't know, I may still be wanted back in Kansas, but that's not because I'm an outlaw."

"Yeah, we know," Gid said. "I wonder if the war will ever be over for us, at least in Kansas."

"I seen 'em," Perry Hoy said. "They got Bell with 'em, 'n looks like they're a' headin' to Jericho."

"Following the tracks, or the creek?"

"Looks like they're followin' the crick."

"Good, I know just the place we can wait for 'em."

"Ha. Bell is goin' to be some surprised when we rescue his ass."

"Bell ain't the only reason we're doin' this. I recognized them two sons of bitches as soon as they started shootin' at us," King said.

"You know them two men? Where'd you know 'em from, because I sure ain't never seen 'em before."

"That's because you wasn't never with Quantrill. I was, 'n that's where I met 'em."

"So you mean they was friends of your'n."

"I wouldn't say they was friends of mine. The last time I seen 'em, they was testifyin' ag'in me in court, 'n that's what got me sent to prison."

"So, we'll shoot 'em down soon as we see 'em," Hoy said.

"No, don't shoot 'em 'less you have to. Bring 'em back to me alive; I wanna make them sons of bitches dance 'fore I let 'em die."

Hoy took three more men with him, and at a gallop, and by cutting through some of the bends of Squaw Creek, they reached a place where a dense growth of trees would provide concealment against anyone coming east, along the creek.

"I seen 'em," Chiles said, coming back to join the other three. "They ain't no more 'n a quarter of mile away, 'n looks like they're just ridin' real slow, 'n talkin' 'n ain't payin' no attention to nothin'.'"

The ride had been a leisurely one, because they didn't want to reopen Bell's wound. They were also in a conversation, and because of their lack of attention and caution, four men suddenly appeared in front of them. All of them were pointing their pistols at Will and Gid.

"We come to rescue you, Bell," one of the men said.

"You know, Perry, I appreciate what you're trying to do, but I've about made up my mind. I'd just as soon go on to jail 'n get this over with," Fred said.

"Now, why 'n hell would you want to do that when we've took this chance like we done to come rescue your ass?" There was a menacing tone to Hoy's words as he pointed his gun at Fred.

Fred smiled, and nodded. "Yeah," he said. "Yeah, that would probably be better anyway." He forced a laugh. "I'd hate to leave before I made any money. What are you going to do with these two?"

"Iffin it was up to me, I'd kill 'em right here 'n now," Hoy said. "But I been told to bring 'em back alive. King knows 'em, 'n he wants to deal with 'em his ownself."

"Old Silas," Will said, perking up at the name. "He never gives up."

"Well, you boys can just have yourselves a good reunion, once we get you back to the camp," Hoy said.

Will and Gid had their arms tied to their waist, and another rope passed under the horse from foot to foot. They were secure in the saddles and weren't about to fall off. They wouldn't be able to gallop away either, because Hoy had assigned two outlaws to hold onto the reins of the brothers' horses, so that they were actually being led back.

They were going east, which meant they would have to pass by the way station. However, any hope that Leah or her father might see them and notify the authorities, was killed when Will saw that they had made a wide swing around Eagle Spring Way Station.

"Well, now," King said, with an evil smile. "If it ain't the Crockett brothers. Hell, I ain't seen you two since when? Oh, yeah, since about two months ago why you two got me sent to prison. I don't reckon you figured on seein' me again so soon, did you?"

"What happened to your beard, King?" Will asked. "You should have kept it, it helped to hide just what an ugly son of a bitch you are."

King stroked his chin. "I took it off while I was in prison, 'n I've decided to keep it off. So, what'd ya think? What with me 'n Bell, 'n you two, why we could all get together 'n it would be just like the good old times when we was ridin' with ole Billy. We sure had fun in them days."

"You have a strange idea of fun," Will said.

"Are you tellin' me you didn't have fun back then?" Silas King asked. "Now, you take Lawrence. Damn me, if I ain't never had me no more fun in my life than what we had in Lawrence."

"There was nothing fun about Lawrence," Gid said.

"Yeah," King said. "Yeah, I remember now. There warn't never no way of a' knowin' but seems to me like you two done what you could to keep the rest of us from havin' fun."

Will recalled that Fred Bell didn't join in the massacre, but like Will and Gid, did what he could to save a few lives, especially some women and children. Will knew for a fact, that Silas King had killed at least two women,

116

and though he didn't see it, others reported that King had also raped a nine-year-old girl before he killed her.

"So what about it, boys? Do you want to join the King Gang?" King asked.

"Not until hell freezes over," Will said resolutely.

King laughed out loud. "I didn't think you would, but I thought I'd ask, just to see if you'd be willin' to join up just to save your hides. Tell the truth, even if you'd said you'd join up, I wouldn't 'a let you. Not after what you two sons of bitches done to me at the trial."

"Now, how 'bout tomorrow I send the both of you to hell, 'n you two can just stay there 'til it freezes over."

"You, Hoy, tie 'em up 'roun' that tree over there," King continued. He was pointing to a sapling that was the only tree that looked strong enough to hold the two of them.

Will and Gid were seated on either side of the tree with their arms pulled behind them so that they were tied to each other, but with the tree separating them.

"How 'we goin' to kill 'em, Silas?" one of the men asked.

"Slow 'n hurtin'," King replied with an evil laugh. "'N we're goin to give 'em all night to be thinkin' about it."

Three hours later the camp was filled with the aroma of bacon, biscuits, and coffee.

"Do you think they'll give us anything to eat?" Gid asked.

"I wouldn't count on it," Will said.

A few minutes later Fred came over carrying two biscuit and bacon sandwiches.

"I was hopin' you wouldn't forget us," Gid said as Bell held the biscuit up for him to take a bite.

"Fred, you aren't really with these people, are you?" Will asked. "I don't remember you being anything like this."

"The truth is, it looks like I've got a bull by the tail," Fred responded. "I got myself in here, and right now I don't see no way of gettin' out."

"Bell!" King called, loudly. "Why the hell are you wastin' food on them two bastards. We're goin' to kill 'em first thing in the mornin', they don't need nothin' to eat."

"Take one last big bite," Fred said quietly, practically shoving the biscuit into Gid's mouth.

"Get your ass back over here!" King shouted. "This ain't no family reunion!"

"Sorry, Will," Fred said, quietly, as with one biscuit still in his hand he started back toward the others.

"You didn't get anything did you?" Gid asked, after Bell left.

"That's all right," Will said. "Looks to me like eating is the least of our worries now."

"I never thought it would end like this," Gid said. "I figured we'd probably get shot down in some gunfight, I never thought about being tied to a tree and getting killed by someone we've known for a long time."

"Yeah, well we aren't dead yet," Will said.

When Will was awakened in the middle of the night, he was surprised, because he wasn't even aware he had fallen asleep.

"Will, Gid wake up, 'n be quiet."

"Fred, what are you doing here?" Will asked.

Bell held out a knife. "I'm going to cut you loose, but you have to be quick and quiet."

"What about our horses?" Gid whispered.

"I'm afraid they're in with the others, and I can't get to them. But here are your guns."

"Fred, we won't forget this," Will said as he and Gid removed the rest of the ropes.

"You'd better not, if I get out of this alive," Fred said.

Will and Gid slipped away, but they hadn't gone more than thirty yards when they heard King's voice.

"Bell, you son of a bitch! You let them bastards go!"

That was followed by a cry of alarm which the brothers recognized as Fred's scream

They heard King's voice. "Get out there 'n find them sons of bitches! They ain't got horses, they couldn't 'a gone far."

"You want us to bring 'em back?" someone asked.

"No, I don't want you to bring 'em back, I want you to

kill 'em," King said.

"We need to get out of here," Gid said.

"No, if we're moving around, they'll find us. We'll stay right here, they won't think of looking for us this close," Will said, his comment, like Gid's, a whisper.

Will and Gid crawled in under some bushes which had the effect of concealing them unless someone got down low enough to the ground to specifically look under the underbrush. And as the searchers were mounted, their hiding place seemed secure. From where they were, they could hear, and occasionally see the men who were searching for them.

Will and Gid's place of concealment was close enough to the encampment that by the light of the fire, they could see what was going on. Bell had been tied to the same tree where Will and Gid had been secured. Fred had been severely beaten, and even in the flickering light of the fire, they could see his face that was now swollen and contorted.

"Gid, we can't let this go on," Will said.

"You're the smart one," Gid said. "Do you have any ideas?"

"No, not yet, but we can't just leave him here."

Every so often King, or one of the others would walk over to Fred and stare down at him. Each visit had some consequence: either a blow to the face, or a kick in the side, opening up his gunshot wound.

Fred grunted loudly or responded with a gasp of pain from the earlier visits, but as the visits got further apart and the night grew longer, they heard nothing more from Fred.

"Will, do you think he's dead?" Gid asked.

"I don't know," Will replied. "Lord help me, I don't know."

The searchers returned to the camp just after dawn.

"We didn't see hide nor hair of 'em," Chiles said.

"Then we can't stay here. If them two get to that way station or even into town, they'll be bringin' the sheriff back with 'em," King said.

"What'll we do with Bell?"

"Is he still alive?" King asked.

"I don't think so," Hoy said. "He sure ain't movin' and he ain't makin' no sound."

"Want me to shoot 'im just to be sure?" Hoy asked.

"Yeah, go ahead 'n shoot . . . no, wait, shootin' is too fast. Leave 'im the way he is if he's breathin'. Either the critters will get 'im, or he'll starve to death."

"What about his horse?" Chiles asked.

"We'll take it with us, 'n the two Crockett horses, too," King said.

"Maybe we can sell 'em, 'n at least get some money out

121

of all this," Baker said.

"Yeah, we sure didn't get nothin' from the train hold up."

"Don't you boys be worryin' none about that," King said. "I got another plan in mind."

Will and Gid overheard the entire conversation, and watched as King and the others broke camp, then got mounted and rode away.

Gid started to go toward the encampment, empty now except for the still form of Fred Bell.

"No, Gid, wait," Will said, putting a hand on his brother's arm to keep him in place. "They might come back."

After about ten minutes, with a nod from Will, they made their way to Fred's body.

"Is he's alive," Gid asked.

"Yes, but just barely," Will said as he felt for a pulse.

"What are we going to do with him?"

"Somehow and don't ask me how, we're going to take him to Eagle Spring. I think that's the closest civilization we're going to find."

Chapter Twelve

"We don't have any horses," Gid said. "How are we going to get him out of here?"

"I don't know," Will said. "I'm afraid if we carry him, we'll just make things worse."

"We can't leave him here, Will; it's like King said, either the critters will get him, or he'll starve to death."

"Yeah, I know but . . . wait a minute, take off your shirt," he said, interrupting his original comment.

"What?"

"Take off your shirt," Will repeated, as he began stripping out of his own shirt. "Then get Fred's while I find a couple of long poles."

A broad smile spread across Gid's face. "Yeah," he said. "Yeah, I know what you're goin' to do. I think that might work."

Searching around the encampment, Will found two

long limbs and after stripping off the branches, he took them back to where Gid had laid out the three shirts. Gid had pulled up some willow shrubs from nearby as well.

Using the sleeves, the two brothers knotted them on the poles, then wove some of the willow branches below the shirts for support, thus creating a crude, but effective travois. Gently, they put Bell on the travois, then started pulling him away, wanting to put as much distance between them and the encampment as they could.

"Do you think he's gonna make it?" Gid asked. "We need to get him to a doctor."

"We can only do so much," Will suggested. "If he lives long enough, we'll get to Eagle Spring before dark and Leah can take a look at him. If she can't do anything, we can put him on a train for Jericho."

"And it will take that much more time before we get back to looking for Julia."

"We don't have any other choice."

"Uhnn!" Fred said, and looking back toward the travois, they saw that some of the support branches had slipped.

"Damn, he's draggin' on the ground," Gid said.

"At least we know he's still alive," Will said. "Let's get some more brush and see if we can do a better job on the travois."

As gingerly as possible, Will and Gid lifted Fred to the

ground and then repaired the travois.

"Let's just pray the shirts don't start ripping," Will said when the weaving was finished and the knots on the shirts strengthened.

"Yeah, I'd hate to have to take off my pants."

With Fred back on the travois, they resumed their travel.

"What are we going to do with him?" Gid asked.

"What do you mean, what are we going to do with him? I told you, we're taking him back to the Eagle Spring way station," Will said.

"No, I mean, after. We were taking him to jail when we got waylaid, but if it hadn't been for Fred, we'd be dead."

"It this was his first raid with King, and nobody actually got hurt, we can speak for him when it comes to trial."

"Yeah," Gid said. "We can at least do that. Maybe he won't get all that much time."

"I'll tell you what I'd like to do," Will said. "I'd like to get hold of Silas King and take his ass back to jail. That'd get us even with him for what he had planned for us, and who knows, there's probably a bigger bounty on him now."

"Yeah," Gid said with a broad grin. "I don't think the state thinks too kindly on jail breakers. But right now, I could eat a horse, I'm so hungry."

"We're making better progress that I expected, so we

could be to Eagle Springs by mid-afternoon," Will said.

"In plenty of time to get something to eat for supper," Gid added. "Or at least maybe Leah has made her bread today."

"I have no doubt Leah will feed us but remember I didn't even get the bacon biscuit that Fred brought to us, and you did."

Outlaw Permanent Camp

The little cabin had been built by an old prospector who had constructed it tight against the weather. It sat fairly close to Devils River, though it was far enough back from the water that even in the deepest spring freshets, it wouldn't be flooded. It was shaded by alamo trees, and at the moment, one of the trees was providing the base for a drumming woodpecker.

Shortly after King and the others returned to their cabin, two new riders arrived.

"Jamie Kincaid," Silas King shouted out to them as they drew within fifty yards of the cabin. "How ya been?"

"Jamie, do you know that man?" Julia asked in a frightened voice.

"Me 'n ole' King here have been friends for a long time," Kincaid said, just as quietly. "We done a few jobs together, back when."

"But don't you know? This is the same man who tried to kidnap me. He's the one who stopped the stagecoach, don't you remember? He doesn't have a beard, but I'd recognize that nose anywhere."

"Of course I remember. How else do you think he knew you was gonna be on that coach in the first place?"

"You told him? You were in on this from the beginning?"

"Sure. I told 'im," Kincaid said with a contemptuous smile. "It's easier'n robbin' a bank."

Julia felt anger welling up inside of her.

"Jamie, I want to go home. I demand it!"

"Why, you little brat. You ain't figured this out yet, have ya? You'll be going home, when your pa pays for you to go home."

Julia set her jaw and held back tears. She was not going to let this man see that she was afraid. She would have to be strong to get through this.

"So, Jamie, workin' on a ranch got a little old did it? You decided to join up with ole' King again?"

"Somethin' like that, yeah," Kincaid replied.

"What the hell did you bring the girl for?" King asked. "What do you plan to do with her?"

"Same thing we was gonna do with her iffen we'd took her off the stage in the first place. We can sell her back to her Papa and we can raise the price," Kincaid said.

"Hell, that ain't all we can do with her," Hoy said, grabbing his crotch.

"No, not yet," King said, sticking out his hand as if holding Hoy back. "If she's going to be any good to us, we'd better keep her just the way we found her. You ain't touched her, have you Kincaid?"

Kincaid laughed. "Not unless you count titties."

"You mean we're gonna have to put up with a damn woman, and we can't touch her?" Baker asked. "King, you sure know how to take the fun out of things."

"If it works out the way Jamie thinks it will, we'll have enough money to have all the whores we want," King said.

"And what if it don't work out? What if her ole' man won't pay nothin' to get her back?"

King smiled.

"Well, in that case, we won't need no whores."

"Who gets to bust her in?" Liddell asked.

"We'll do it fair and square," King said. "We'll draw cards."

"Yeah," Hoy said, and again he grabbed his crotch and made a suggestive thrust toward Julia. "You know what, I damn near hope her ole' man don't pay nothin' for her."

"I'll be first," Kincaid said. "I'm the one that brung 'er. Besides," he added, looking at Julia with a salacious grin. "This little girl loves me. Don't you, honey?"

Julia spat. "How could I ever love someone like you?"

128

"Let me remind you, girly, I didn't come up to your room and snatch you out'a your bed. You come right down all by your ownself."

"Kincaid's right. He'll be first just to get her tamed down. Hell, as much as a spitfire as she is, she might bite." King reached up to rub the lower half of his nose."

"Speakin' of, have ya got 'nything to eat?" Kincaid asked. "There ain't neither one of us et nothin' since yesterday mornin'."

"We got bacon 'n beans in the pot," King said. "I suppose we could all eat, now."

"What do you want to do with her?" Kincaid asked.

"Bring her on inside, we'll tie 'er up, to the leg of the heatin' stove. We ain't needin' it and she sure as hell won't drag that off. Just make sure she's tied good and tight, so's she can't work the knot loose."

Julia looked at Jamie, then at the other men who had come out of the cabin to leer at her. The horror of her situation was so terrifying, that it almost became mind numbing. What was going to happen to her? She wasn't sure what they meant by, 'taking their turns with her' but she had an idea, and it was too horrible to contemplate.

"I gotta take a piss," one the men said. Piss wasn't a word Julia normally heard, though she had heard some of her father's hands use it from time to time when they didn't know she was close enough to hear.

The man who had declared his intention stepped just outside the door of the little cabin and began urinating.

Seeing him, Julia closed her eyes, and looked away.

"Baker, you dumb son of a bitch, ain't you go no better sense than to take a piss right in front of the door?" one of the others asked.

"What difference does it make where I pee? I ain't doin' it in the house."

"Well, we're fixin' to eat 'n nobody wants to eat where somebody's been takin' a piss."

"Beans again?"

"You don't want 'em, I'll eat your share."

"No, now there ain't no need for you to do nothin' like that. I'll eat 'em."

Inside the cabin the men, whose names Julia would soon learn as Val Baker, Frog Jones, Andy Liddell, and Spider Murray were seated around the table. Silas King, as was his due, was sitting at the head of the table. Perry Hoy and Kit Chiles, and Jamie Kincaid joined them.

Julia was given a spoon and a tin pan filled with beans that, as only one of her legs was tied to the stove, she placed on her knees. Never in her life would she have thought she would be subjected to such humiliation, but she knew she would have to eat to stay alive.

"Boss, we got to get us some money," Frog Jones said.

"This here is damn near the end of the beans, 'n it is the end of the bacon."

"I've got somethin' in mind," King replied.

"Oh, yeah, we're goin' to ransom the girl back to her ole' man."

"No, not yet," King said. "If we hold her a little longer, Abernathy'll ante up a pretty penny."

"So, what's on your mind? Hittin' another train?"

"No, you can't always control what's goin' on around you. You never know what might crop up."

"You mean like the Crocketts?"

"Hmmph" King grunted.

"I've done pretty good holdin' up stagecoaches," Murray said.

King shook his head. "Naw, it ain't hardly worth the effort anymore. It's mostly trains that carry the money now."

"Then if we ain't talkin' about robbin' a train, or holdin' up a stagecoach, what are you talking about?" Jones asked.

King smiled. "Well, where do you think the trains is carryin' that money from?"

"Well, I reckon they's a' carryin' it from a bank. Son of a bitch, you're talkin' about holdin' up a bank, ain't ya? I don't know if that's such a good idea though. I mean you go into a town like Jericho, or San Antonio, or El Paso, they got sheriffs 'n deputies just waitin' for you."

"They's other towns. I know one that's only got one town marshal, and he's so old, he don't hardly know which way's up," King said. "But it's got a bank, just full of money for the takin'."

Now it was Chiles time to smile. "Then let's do it."

Chapter Thirteen

Eagle Spring:

It was late afternoon by the time Will and Gid, pulling Fred Bell on the improvised travois, reached the Eagle Spring way station. Leah, who was standing at the well drawing up a bucket of water, was startled by the unexpected appearance of two shirtless men pulling what looked like a man lying on an improvised travois.

Upon closer examination, she recognized the two men as the Crockett brothers. But where were their horses and why were they coming from the southwest, when they had left here going northeast?

The man on the travois looked to have been badly beaten, but she recognized him as Fred Bell, the young man who had been shot in the attempted train robbery.

"Oh, my!" she said as they drew close enough for conversation. "What happened?"

"Leah, I'm afraid we're going to need a little more of your nursing," Will said.

"Of course, get him inside, quickly!"

Gid reached down, scooped Fred up in his arms and carried him inside with ease.

"Put him on the same bed," Leah said, pointing to the bed her patient had occupied the time before.

Shortly after Bell was laid out on the bed, he opened his eyes and saw Leah. A smile spread across his face, but he couldn't speak.

"Where's Mr. Godfrey?" Will asked.

"Papa left on the morning train. He wanted to make sure the sheriff knew what happened out here with those two dead men, but he'll be back on the last train."

"While we wait, have you got anything to eat," Gid asked.

"Gid!" Will spoke the name in a chastising tone of voice.

"Are you hungry now?" Leah asked.

"Yes, ma'am, I haven't had anything to eat since we left here and I truly am hungry."

Leah smiled. "Would some cold flapjacks hold you over until Papa gets back?"

"Yes, ma'am, that would be very nice of you. Even better if you had a little jam."

Half an hour later as Will and Gid were finishing

their impromptu meal of rolled up flapjacks, Leah had gotten Fred cleaned up and was now forcing some warm tea down him.

"I thank you, ma'am," Fred said, his voice barely above a whisper.

Leah smiled. "If you're going to be here for a while, call me Leah."

"Yes, ma'am."

"Leah"

"All right, it's Leah and I'm Fred."

The telegraph began clattering and Leah hurried over to it, keyed a response, then sat by the device taking down the message that was being sent.

"You can do that?" Gid asked after the message was completed, surprised to see her handle the key.

"Yes, that's our main job here," Leah replied. "This message will be passed on to the engineer of the next southwest-bound train." Her comment was punctuated by the whistle of an incoming train.

"And it got here just in time," she added.

"Which way is this train going?" Will asked.

"Southwest."

"That won't do."

Putting the message on the end of a long pole, Leah went out to wait for the train.

"She's some kind of a lady," Fred said, his voice a little

stronger after drinking the tea.

"She's been taking good care of you all right," Will said.

"But it's more than that. She's nice and she's real smart. Did you see how she handled that telegraph key."

"You know what, Big Brother, I think our friend, Fred, here, is smitten," Gid said. "What do you think?"

"Maybe I am, but it can't go anywhere. I'm an outlaw." Fred let out a long sigh and turned his head.

"Let's talk about this outlaw business for a moment," Will said. "Are you telling the truth when you say that when King hit the train yesterday, it was your very first time? Or are you just saying something you think Gid and I would like to hear?"

"Well, I can't say it's the first time, but it's the first time since the war."

"What we did during the war doesn't count," Gid said. "Or at least it doesn't in my mind."

"I know you're going to have to take me on into jail, but could you wait just a few days? Until I get back on my feet a little more," Fred asked. "I don't want to go to jail just yet, because I can barely move."

They heard the train leaving then and a moment later Leah and her father, came in.

"Mr. Godfrey," Will said. "I guess you didn't expect to see us so soon."

"Well I thought you might be back through here. I have

something for you."

"Oh?" Will questioned.

Buck reached down into the satchel he was carrying and took out an envelope. "It turns out that there was a reward of two hundred dollars each on the two men you killed. I was authorized to bring the four hundred dollars to you."

"Well that was unexpected," Will said. "Thank you."

"Yeah, especially since we don't have a red cent between us. King took all our money when we were prisoners," Gid said.

"Leah was telling me what happened to you." Buck looked over toward Fred. "How are you doin', young man?"

"Better than I have any right to be, thanks to Will 'n Gid saving me and the nursing I'm getting from your daughter."

"You might do even better if you had something to eat, wouldn't you?" Buck asked with a smile.

"They've already eaten," Leah said.

"Eaten? Well now, Miss Leah, don't get me wrong, those flapjacks were delicious but I sort of figured that was just eating something while we were waiting to eat," Gid said.

Leah laughed. "Don't worry, it's about supper time and I've had some soup on all afternoon. All I need to do now is make some cornbread and we'll be all set. That won't take long."

Later, with nothing remaining in his bowl, Fred wiped his mouth on a napkin. "I tell you the truth, Leah, as pretty as you are, and as good as you can nurse and cook, you're going to make someone an awfully good wife."

"Are you proposing to my daughter, young man?" Buck asked.

"Papa!" Leah gasped, but Buck's laugh let her know that he was only teasing.

"When is the next southwest-bound train?" Will asked.

"Tomorrow morning. Why do you want to know?" Buck asked.

"If you recall, we were going to El Paso, when we were interrupted." Will said. "We still need to get to El Paso. We're looking for a rancher's missing daughter and I feel guilty that we've been sidetracked."

"Stopping a train robbery is a little more than just being sidetracked," Buck said. "I suspect the Texas and Pacific might pony up a little appreciation money for you two. Especially when I tell them what happened to you."

"That would be nice, but it's not necessary. Right now, we have to get on with our business. Mr. Godfrey," Will started, but Godfrey interrupted him.

"It's Buck."

"All right, Buck, we need a couple of things. First my brother and I need some new gear since King and his gang have ours and second, would it be all right if Fred stayed here until we get back? He should be recovered enough by then, that we can take him back to the sheriff."

"It's all right with me," Buck said. "That is if it's all right with Leah."

"It's fine," Leah said as she brushed a lock of Fred's hair off his forehead.

The next morning, Buck and the Crocketts were outside waiting for the train. "Tell me boys, how well do you know this Bell?" Buck asked.

"As well as you know anybody in a war situation," Will said. "We rode with him off and on for two years. When the war was over, he went his way and we went ours."

"He seems like a nice fellow. Wonder how he got mixed up in this outlaw gang?" Buck asked.

"You'll have to ask him about that," Gid said. "I believe him when he says it was the first time, he did something that was against the law. Why do you ask?"

"You see Leah fussin' with him. I worry about her out here all by herself. Don't know what would become of her if somethin' was to happen to me," Buck said.

"Well, if it's any comfort to you, if Fred goes to trial, Gid and I intend to testify on his behalf. He's in the shape he's in, because he saved our lives, and he knew what would happen to him. In my book, that's worth something."

Buck nodded his head. "Train's comin'."

When Will and Gid got on the El Paso bound train, it turned out the same conductor was on the train.

"Mr. Gillespie," Will said as he shook the conductor's hand, "I wonder if my brother and I could continue our trip to El Paso?"

Gillespie smiled at the two brothers. "Since the two of you saved the train from being robbed, that's the least we can do."

"Thanks, Bill," Gid said as they made their way to the same seats they had occupied before their previous trip was interrupted.

"I feel a little guilty about this," Gid said as the train got underway.

"Guilty about what? Getting free passage for the rest of the way to El Paso?"

"No, I feel guilty because we aren't already there, searching for Julia. We should have been there long before now."

"I know, Little Brother, but we couldn't help it. If Julia is in El Paso, and if she's with Kincaid, she probably won't be exactly happy to see us."

"In a way, I hope you're right. Maybe they did get married. Then what are we going to do?"

"We'll try to convince them both to come back with us. If they are married like Julia said she wanted to do in her note, maybe John can learn to accept Kincaid as a son-in-law," Will said.

"And I have no doubt that Kincaid can accept John as a father-in-law, especially when he thinks about all the money John has," Gid said. "Now where did John say we should go first, once we get to El Paso?"

"He found out Kincaid used to work for the El Paso Warehouse where he loaded and unloaded freight cars. John said the man we should see is named Wyatt. Ralph Wyatt. He owns the place and he remembered Kincaid."

"All right, that's the first place we'll go when we get there," Gid said.

"The warehouse will more than likely be closed by the time we get there. Tonight we'll find a place to stay and have supper, then we'll visit a couple of the saloons and who knows, we might just get lucky and find Kincaid in one of 'em. If you remember, Jamie really liked the ladies and it's hard to think he'd change his ways, just because he married Julia."

Gid shook his head. "What do you think made Julia fall in with this son of a bitch?"

Chapter Fourteen

After having supper at The Red Hen restaurant, the two brothers began to tour the saloons, limiting themselves to one beer in each of them. There were ten saloons, but after the fourth one, the beers just sat before them, untouched. They wanted to make certain they kept their wits about them.

They weren't sure what the best way to ask about Jamie Kincaid was, so they just came out and ask their casual encounters if anyone had ever heard of him. Getting nothing but negative responses from the men, they began to concentrate on the bar girls. They got lucky in the Bit and Bridle, the sixth saloon they visited.

"Why do you ask about Jamie Kincaid?" one of the bar girls asked.

"You know him?"

"I know him."

"From the tone of your voice, it doesn't sound like you have all that good of an impression of him."

"He's a pig," the bargirl who had identified herself as Mabel said.

"Why do you call my friend a pig?" Will asked, having introduced all his queries with the suggestion that they were friends and he was just trying to reconnect with him.

"If he's your friend, you know why I say he's a pig. The way he ran away like he did."

"Ran away? Ran away from you?"

Mabel pointed to one of the girls, leaning over a table of two men, flirting outrageously. "From her," Mabel said.

"What's her name?"

"In here she goes by Polly, but her real name is Evaline. Evaline Kincaid."

"Kincaid? Is she his sister?"

"No, she's his wife," Maggie said.

"His wife. I had no idea."

Will walked over to the girl.

"Polly?"

"Butt out, mister, Polly's busy," one of the men said.

"I'm sorry," Will said. "Are these gentlemen paying for your company?"

"No," Polly said. "What can I do for you, honey?"

"How much does it cost to go up to your room with you?"

"Three dollars for a short visit, Five dollars for all night."

"All right, I'll give you five dollars."

One of the two men who had been sitting at the table stood up. He was a big man, about the size of Gid. "Mister, you can't just come in here and take away our girl like that."

"Oh? I thought it was her business to entertain men who paid her. And from the looks of things, I don't think you're paying her a thing," Will said.

The other man at the table stood as well, and though he wasn't as big as the first man, he was a good-sized man.

"What if we don't want you to take her?" the second man asked.

"Are you having a problem here, Big Brother?" Gid asked.

Gid's appearance startled the two men who thought they had the opportunity to buffalo this stranger who had interrupted their conversation with the bar girl.

"I don't think these gentlemen fully understand the concept of Miss Polly's business," Will said. "She sells her time and she and I have entered into a verbal contract. I've already tendered the funds necessary to close the deal."

"That sounds reasonable to me," Gid said. "I'm sure it does to the two of you as well."

Suddenly and with no warning, the bigger of the two men took a swing at Gid, thinking that by taking him down, they could intimidate Will.

Gid caught the big man's fist in his hand, then began squeezing, squeezing so hard that the big man cried out, then sank to his knees in pain.

When the other man at the table saw how easily the big man had handled his friend, he started for his gun, but in a move so fast that nobody saw it, Will had his gun in his hand.

"I think we can finish this discussion now, don't you?"

The man nodded.

"Give me your gun," Will said. "As a matter of fact, both of you give me your guns."

"Mister, you ain't got no right to take our guns. That's stealin'."

"Oh, I would prefer to say I'm just borrowing them. I'm going upstairs with Miss Polly now and when she and I have concluded our business, I'll give them to the bartender in the morning."

"What do you mean, in the morning?"

"You don't understand morning? It means that in a little bit, it's going to get all dark outside but after awhile, it will be light again because the sun will come up. And when it does, well, we call that morning." Will explained morning as if he were explaining it to a child and those who were close enough to overhear what was being said, laughed aloud.

The two men glared at Will.

"What do you say Miss Polly, shall we go upstairs?" Will asked.

Polly, appeared to be somewhat shaken by the sudden activity that went on around her so Will, after giving the two pistol belts to Gid, put his hand on her shoulder in a calming, and reassuring way.

"Don't be frightened, I'm sure there will be no more trouble," he said.

"Are you some kind of lawyer," Polly asked.

"No, why do you ask?"

"Because of the way you talk," Polly said as she started for the stairs.

Gid found a table and kept an eye on the two men who had challenged his brother. For the moment, the two he was watching were sulking quietly.

Outlaw cabin

"Someone has to stay with the girl," King said. "And, Kincaid, since you brung her out here, that'll be you."

"He won't be gettin' no share of the money, will he?" Hoy asked.

"He's part of the outfit, so he'll get a share," King insisted.

"That don't hardly seem none to fair to me," Hoy said.

"We're the ones robbin' the bank, 'n he gets to stay here with the girl."

"He's also the one that brought the girl, so he is the best one to stay behind."

"No tellin' what he'll be doin' with her while we're all gone," Hoy said.

"He knows that if we're goin' to get any money from her pappy, then he can't do nothin' to her."

"Yeah? Well, still it don't seem right for him to get a share from the bank but he don't do nothin' for it."

"Are you askin' for a share of the ransom we'll get for the girl?" King asked.

"Well, yeah."

"Why? You didn't do anythin' to get her here."

"All right," Hoy said.

"Then let's get movin'. I want to get there just after the bank opens, so's there's not a lot of customers," King said.

Julia listened to the sound of the horses hoof falls as everyone but Jamie rode off. She was sitting behind the stove with her back up against the wall. Her ankle was still tied, but now her wrists were bound as well. She was able to move enough to lie down on the floor and someone had given her a single dirty blanket to sleep on.

What bothered her more than anything else, was that she was here by her own volition. She had run away in the middle of the night because she thought she wanted to be with Jamie Kincaid.

She realized now how foolish she was. Her parents, especially her father, had done everything he could to rule against her, but she wouldn't listen to him. Now, she had no idea if she would ever get out of this mess. She only knew, she had made a terrible mistake.

She looked over at Jamie, who was still standing in the door looking out toward the men who were riding away.

"Those sons of bitches better give me my share," he said, more to himself than to Julia.

"Jamie?" Julia said in a small, plaintive voice.

"What do you want?" Kincaid asked, his voice very nearly a snarl.

"Jamie, why are you doing this? You know that I thought I loved you. You never did anything to discourage me."

"Why should I have done that?"

"Jamie, what's going to happen to me?"

"What do you mean what's going to happen to you? I've told you, we're going to ransom you back to your old man."

"Does Papa know where I am?"

"Hell if I know," Jamie said. "Silas is the boss."

"Will he let the others . . ." Julia couldn't finish the sentence.

"King says no. Now, don't bother me."

"Would it bother you if they . . . if they had their way with me?" The thought of it was so horrible, that she could barely ask the question.

"No, why should it bother me?"

"Jamie?"

"What?" Jamie replied.

Julia looked at Jamie. No, this wasn't the Jamie she thought she knew and she would never again think of him as so. This was Kincaid.

Jamie came back into the cabin and sat at the table eating a hard biscuit that was left behind after the men had gone. He picked up a newspaper that was on the table and stared at it for a long time. After a while he spoke.

"Can you read?"

"Of course I can. That's why you took us to school every day," Julia said.

"Then read this to me." He pointed to an article, as he held the paper in front of her face.

Julia began to read the article.

Failed Train Robbery Attempt

On the fifth, Instant, the El Paso limited out of Ft. Worth was stopped at the Eagle Spring Way Station when it was hit upon by several outlaws, said to be led by the recently escaped, Silas King.

The attempted hold up was thwarted because of the action of two men, the brothers Crockett, Will and Gid.

"Will and Gid Crockett," Kincaid said aloud. "Those bastards! They're the same ones who caused us trouble before. If they'd let us take you from the stage, we'd have our money already and you'd be back sassin' your papa."

"Will and Gid? They're coming here?" Julia asked with some hope in her voice."

"Ha!" Kincaid replied. "There ain't no way they're goin' to come here, unless they're ready to die."

Julia was quiet for a few more minutes, then she spoke again. "Jamie, could you untie me, please? I have to, uh, go outside."

"Go ahead, pee if you have to."

"Where?"

"Right where you are. Pee in your pants."

"Don't make me do that," she pleaded. "When King is here, I get to go outside. Why won't you let me go now?"

"Cause when the gang's here, there weren't no chance you'd run away."

"There's no way I can run away and you know it. Please, if you ever had one good thought about me before, untie me and let me go pee."

"All right," Kincaid said as he united Julia's hands and

feet. He drew his pistol, then waved it toward the door. "You find yourself a tree somewhere, but if you try and run, I won't come after you. I'll just shoot you."

El Paso

Polly led Will into her room, then closed the door. She forced a smile, then started to untie her bodice, but Will held out his hand.

"There's no need for that," he said.

Will's words gave Polly a confused look.

"You don't want to . . ." she held her arm out toward the bed.

"I want to talk to you about something."

The look of confusion turned to one of agitation. "Are you a newspaper man, wanting to write some salacious story about the women in my profession?"

"Salacious story? You have a very good vocabulary."

"You mean for a whore?" Polly said.

"No, I meant that as a sincere compliment. I have a unique situation here. I've been paid by a man to find his sixteen-year-old daughter. She was taken from him by . . . no, to be truthful, she ran away of her own free will with . . ."

"Jamie Kincaid," Polly finished in a voice without emotion.

"That's right," Will said. "I understand that you were once his wife."

"I'm still his wife," Polly replied.

"Does he ever come around?"

"I've seen him a couple of times."

"Well, I'm looking for him and if I find him, I think I'll find the girl as well."

"Not necessarily," Polly said.

"What do you mean, not necessarily?"

"I mean if he can find someone who'll buy her from him, he'll sell her," Polly said. "That's what he does."

"Have you any idea where he might be?"

"I don't know where he is, I just know where he isn't. He isn't in El Paso or someone would have told me by now," Polly said. "I have friends all over town who know him and they all know what he did to me."

"If I'm not being too nosy, what did he do to you?" Will asked.

"He didn't do it to me. Like the girl you're looking for, I did it to myself," Polly said.

"I was a student at Chapel Hill Female College. My father wanted me to get an education, then come back home and handle his church. Some people preach the gospel to save souls and some do it to make money. My father was making a lot of money. My mama was dead and he thought someone with a business degree would help him make even more money."

"Chapel Hill Female College, like any good Texas school, had a stable where we learned to ride, side-saddle, as ladies are supposed to. The person who managed the livery was Jamie Kincaid."

"He was a handsome man, all right and he knew all the right things to say and do to entice a young woman who had always lived a very sheltered life."

Polly hesitated.

"Sort of like how he enticed the girl I'm looking for," Will said.

"I hope it's not as bad as what happened to me. He made me pregnant, and when he found out, he took me to a quack who gave me what he called female pills. They were a concoction of tansy oil, pennyroyal, rue, ergot and opium."

"Anyway, whatever they were, they cause me to lose the baby. When my father found out he said he wouldn't be able to have me around his church." She laughed. "No place for a fallen woman. Anyway he gave me five hundred dollars and told me he never wanted to see me again."

"Then there was Jamie. He was so kind and solicitous and he asked me to marry him. We opened a bank account and I deposited the five hundred dollars my father had given me."

"After a while, the bank account was cleared out and

Jamie Kincaid was gone and my father, the good Christian man that he was, made sure everyone knew what I had done." She stopped again. "And that's when I turned to this." She pointed to the bed, and though she wasn't weeping aloud, tears were tracking down her face.

Will felt compassion for Polly and he walked over to take her in his arms. She looked toward the bed, and when Will released her, she lay down on the bed. Her eyes were big and inviting. Will lay down beside her and held her in his arms.

Chapter Fifteen

When Will went downstairs the next morning, the bar was open, but the only beverage being offered was coffee. The man behind the bar wasn't the same one who had been tending bar last night.

"Are you Will Crockett?" the bartender asked as he poured a cup of coffee for Will.

"I am."

"I was told to give you this note."

Will took the note.

Big Brother,
Since you didn't come down as soon as I thought you would, I figured you decided to spend the night with Polly, so I spent the night with Mabel. If you got this note, wait for me. I'll be down and we can get breakfast.
Gid

Will was on his second cup of coffee when Gid came down the stairs.

"There you are," Will said when he saw his brother.

"Did you have any luck, with Polly?" Gid asked.

"Depends on what you call luck. I found out Kincaid is married."

"Married? Does she know his wife?"

"I'd say so. It's her."

"Oh dear, this could get interesting, but before you tell me, I'm ready for breakfast."

"I thought you might be."

Leaving the saloon, Will and Gid went down the street to a restaurant called The Chatterbox.

Will had bacon and eggs, a biscuit and some coffee. Gid had a stack of pancakes, three eggs, sausage and a rasher of bacon.

"What do we do now?" Gid asked around a mouth full of pancakes.

"So far, Polly has been our only legitimate lead. And she and Kincaid have been separated for four years," Will said. "I think all we can do now is send John a telegram, telling him that Julia isn't in El Paso, but we'll keep looking."

"Where?" Gid asked.

"Right now, I don't have an idea in hell. But, for now, I think we should go back to Eagle Spring and take Fred Bell in. Somebody has to have seen Kincaid and Julia. They can't lay low forever."

On the Green River, near Commerce, Texas

After a ride of about two hours since leaving the cabin, Silas King and the others of his gang stopped at the bridge that crossed Green River. Dismounting, King and Baker walked down to the bank of the river to examine the bridge.

"Do we have enough sticks of dynamite to take the bridge down?" King asked.

"Yeah, easy," Baker replied.

"Where will you put it?"

Baker pointed. "Right there in the middle. Do you see that brace under the bridge? That's where I'll be a' puttin' it. And once it goes, the whole bridge will go."

"It's only about half a mile to town," King said. "Jones and Liddell, you two stay here with Baker. When you see us comin' back, you two shoot at anyone who might be chasin' us. Baker, you wait 'till we actually get on the bridge, then light the fuse. Me, Hoy, Liddell, Murray and Chiles, will be the ones that rides into town. And boys, after we've hit the bank and start ridin' out of town, you start shootin' to keep ever' one's head down."

"How much money you reckon they got in that little ole bank?" Hoy asked.

"How much do you have now?" King asked.

"I ain't got but about three dollars."

"Then what the hell do you care how much money they got? It's for damn sure the bank's got more 'n three dollars," King said.

Hoy and the others laughed.

"You got the dynamite in place?" King asked Baker who had been working under the bridge.

"Just about. Just have to get this fuse strung."

"You got to be just right on this now, don't be too early 'n don't be too late."

"I've used powder and dynamite before," Baker said. "That was my job when I worked in the mines."

"I know it was, that's why I chose you."

King pinched off the end of his quirley, then tossed the butt away. "All right, boys, let's go get some money," he said as he got mounted.

It was about nine o'clock in the morning and with all the stores opening, the citizens of the small town were going about their business. Two old men were playing checkers in front of the Commerce Feed and Seed Store. One of the two men was stroking his chin as he stared at the checker board.

"You got to take your jump, J.R.," the other player said.

"I'm ponderin' on it."

"There ain't no ponderin' to it, you got to take your jump."

"Lem is right, J.R.," one of the kibitzers said. "You got to take your jump, you ain't got no choice in it."

J.R. took the jump, then with a triumphant chuckle, Lem jumped four of J.R.s men.

"Now you see," J.R. said, pointing to the checkerboard. "That there is exactly why I didn't want to take that jump."

Lem laughed. "'N that there's why you had to take it."

In an open lot between the barbershop and the leather-goods shop, a couple of boys were tossing horse shoes.

The loud clank of one of the shoes hitting the stob elicited a shout of excitement from one of two boys.

"Ha! I got me a ringer, Jimmy Ray! Did you see how it was spinnin' around, then just dropped down like it done?"

"You got lucky, Roy, that's all," Jimmy Ray replied.

"Huh uh, it warn't luck, I'm just about the bestest horse shoe thrower there is," Roy replied.

Across the street from the game of checkers and the two boys throwing horse shoes, a woman and a young girl were standing on the board walk out in front of The Dress Shoppe, looking at the display window.

"Mama, you should buy that dress," the little girl said. "You would look so pretty in it."

Marylou Patterson smiled at her daughter. "Thank you, Amy, but sweetheart I'm afraid that dress cost more money than I can afford."

A buckboard sat in front of Raferty's Grocery Store and an older woman was standing alongside her white-haired husband while he was loading the groceries in the back.

"Clem, did you get me some Persil bleach? I can't be gettin' your clothes clean without I have me some Persil bleach."

"I got the bleach, Doris," Clem replied as he continued to load his purchases into the buckboard.

"Folks is always sayin' I get my clothes the cleanest, 'n it's because I use me some Persil bleach in with the soap I render out. You sure you got it?"

"I'm sure," Clem said.

"I been a' lookin' at ever' one, 'n it don't look to me like there ain't nobody to be a'worryin' about," Hoy said, as he and the other four men came riding into town.

"Yeah, well, we need to scope 'em all out real good," King said. "I wouldn't want none of the people that's here in town doin' nothin' that we wasn't expectin'."

Two men were sitting on a bench in front of the apothecary when they saw the five men coming into town, all riding together.

"You recognize any o' them boys, Clyde?" Drury Green asked.

Clyde expectorated a quid of tobacco, then wiped his mouth with the back of his hand before he replied.

"More 'n likely some new hands for Gerry Swain. I heard he was puttin' some more on."

"Yeah, I reckon they could be. But tell me this, Clyde, if Gerry Swain just put 'em on, why is it that they'd all be a' comin' into town at the same time? I don't know; I got me some sort of a strange feelin' about this."

Nobody else paid any particular attention to the five men. If they even noticed them at all, they assumed, like Clyde, that they were probably ranch hands from one of the nearby ranches.

The cow hands were a mixed blessing. Sometimes they would get a little rambunctious on Saturday night, but it was a small price to pay for the economic benefit the town received from the ranchers and their hands.

As King into town, he studied both sides of Center Street. He saw the checker players, the boys who were throwing horse shoes, the man and woman behind the buckboard, the woman and her daughter in front of the dress shop, as well as the two men sitting on the bench. He had a close look at everyone else on both sides of the street and saw that the only ones wearing pistols, were the two men in front of the apothecary. King doubted if either one of them could actually use the guns they were carrying.

"Hoy, Liddell, you got them two that's packin' on your side?" King asked just loudly enough for the two men to hear him.

"We see 'em," Hoy answered. He chuckled. "They're just sittin' on their ass, 'n it don't neither one of 'em look like they could get guns out of their holsters without shootin' themselves in the foot."

"Chiles, Murray, do you see any armed men on your side?"

"Ain't nobody that I see so far," Chiles said.

"Remember, when we ride out of here, start shootin' to keep ever' one's head down," King said. "Try not to kill anybody, 'less you have to."

The building they were headed for was at the far end of the street, and it was different from any of the other buildings in town, in that it was the only one made of brick. The name *Bank and Savings Trust of Commerce* was painted in gold outlined black letters on the glass of the front door.

"All right, me, Chiles, 'n Murray will go in," King said when they stopped in front of the bank. "Hoy, you hold my horse, and Liddell, you hold the other two. Iffen there's any shootin' as to be done 'n the horses gets skittish, you hold on to 'em good. I don't want to come out here 'n find my horse gone, cause if that was to happen, I'd shoot the two of you 'n take one of your'n."

"Your horse will be here, I can promise you that," Hoy said.

"Hey, Clyde, don't you think that's some peculiar, that three o' them fellers is dismountin' in front of the bank like that, while them other two is still mounted, 'n holdin' on to all the horses?"

"Yeah, it does look a little strange, don't it?" Clyde admitted.

"Where's Gleason 'n the others?"

"They're in the feed store."

"Let's go in 'n see 'em. Like I told you a while ago, I got me a itchy feelin' 'bout this."

When King, Chiles, and Murray stepped into the bank, they saw only two people, the teller and a middle-aged woman in front of the counter.

"I'll be right with you, gentlemen," the teller called out to them. "You won't have to wait long."

"I don't reckon we want to wait at all," King said. "You'll be with us right now."

"Look here, sir, there is a customer in front of . . ."

King pulled his pistol and brought it crashing down on the woman's head. She collapsed without a word, and blood began to pool on the floor under her head.

"There ain't no one in front of me, now," King said.

"My God, what have you done?" the teller shouted in shock and terror.

"It looks to me like I moved up in your damn line," King said. He pointed his pistol at the teller. "Now, let's get down to business. Give me all the money you got. Give him the bag," King said to Chiles, without giving away his name.

Chiles walked over to the window and stuck the bag through.

"Y . . . yes, sir," the teller replied, as with trembling hands he took the money from the drawers and dropped it into the bag.

"From the safe too," King ordered.

"I'm afraid I don't know the combination to the safe."

"You don't need no combination, it ain't shut," Chiles said with a nod toward the vault, where the door was standing open.

"Oh," the teller said, realizing he had just been caught in a lie.

"Let's go," Chiles said with a little wave of his pistol.

The bank teller walked over to the safe then began pulling stacks of bills from inside and dropping them into the bag.

"That's all of it," the teller said as he handed the bag to King.

"You done good," King said. "I almost hate to have to do this."

King shot the teller in the stomach, then, holding the bag of money, he, Murray and Chiles ran out of the bank, mounted their horses and began riding at a gallop, heading out of town.

As they left town they began shooting indiscriminately at people on both sides of the road. Clem, the white-haired old man who had been loading groceries, went down, and his wife who had been looking toward the galloping riders, screamed in terror and grief.

Roy and Jimmy Ray left the horse shoe pit and stepped out to the edge of the street to see what was going on. One bullet came so close to them that both of them turned and ran toward the alley.

The checker players, J.R. and Lem, as well as Hank, the kibitzer, dived for the porch as a bullet hit the checker board.

"Amy!" Marylou called, and she grabbed her daughter and turned around with her back toward the street, protecting Amy with her own body. Two of the bullets hit the display window, causing it to come crashing down. Marylou pulled Amy closer to her.

"Bank holdup! The bank has been robbed!" someone shouted.

"Son of a bitch, I know'd somethin' wasn't right about them fellers," Drury Green said. "Let's get after 'em!"

Drury, Clyde, Gleason and three others who had ridden in from the Double T Ranch that morning, still had saddled horses right in front of the feed and seed store. The six of them got mounted and galloped out in pursuit of the bank robbers, who by then were just leaving the town limits.

Being hotly pursued, King and the others reached the bridge across Green River within two minutes after leaving town and Baker, who saw them coming, got ready to light the fuse.

"Now! Get that thing lit!" King shouted as he and the other four men arrived, the horse hooves drumming loudly on the wooden floor of the bridge.

Baker touched the match to the fuse and it began sputtering, working its way down, quickly. Baker scurried to get out of the way.

Less than ten seconds after King and his men crossed the river, Drury, Clyde, Gleason and the other three who were in pursuit, rode out onto the bridge. Not until they were on the bridge did one of them see the sparking fuse.

"*Drury, the . . .*" Clyde shouted in warning, but that

166

was as far as he got before the three dynamite sticks went up in a huge explosion. Large pieces of the bridge were driven up by the explosion and all six of the men were caught up in the blast.

When the smoke and shards of wood came settling back down, six horses were in the river. Three of the men, caught under their horses, were still and quiet. Two of the men had managed to pull themselves ashore, but they were lying there moaning, and offered no danger.

The sixth man was nowhere to be seen.

"Oh, sumbitch that was some powerful!" King shouted, gleefully. Then, turning his horse away, he spoke to the others. "Let's head for the river."

Chapter Sixteen

El Paso

The train had arrived a few minutes earlier and now sat in front of the depot poised for the continuation of it journey. With the expelling rhythmic gushes of steam, smoke curling up from the stack, bearings and couplings popping and snapping as they cooled, it was as if the engine were some living creature, drawing and expelling breaths.

As Will and Gid stood on the platform they were assailed with several smells. Most prominent was the aroma of spicy meat being cooked for the tacos that the vendors were offering for sale, competing with the smell of coal smoke. And though the cattle holding pens were some distance away from the passenger depot, the stench of the enclosed animals could also be detected.

The telegram they had sent to John, expressing regret for not having found Julia in El Paso had already been answered.

PLEASE CONTINUE SEARCH WHEREVER IT MIGHT LEAD

JOHN

Although they had no information that led to Eagle Spring, that was where they were headed.

"We have to be somewhere," Will had told Gid. "And right now, I choose to be at Eagle Spring."

"We're going after King, aren't we?" Gid asked.

"I think we may as well," Will said. "It will give us something to do while we try to sniff out where to go next to look for Julia and Kincaid."

"Fred might have an idea where we can start looking for King."

"My thought, exactly."

"'BOARD!" the conductor called. Will was disappointed to see that it wasn't Bill Gillespie.

The two brothers stepped up into the train, then took their seats in one of the day cars. It would be a six-hour trip to Eagle Spring if all went well.

Outlaw Cabin:

Back at the cabin, Julia heard the men shouting and

laughing as they returned.

"Sounds like it must've gone pretty good, don't it?" Kincaid said.

Julia cringed at Kincaid's grammar. Why hadn't she noticed that before?

Kincaid went outside to welcome the return of King and the others, and Julia was thankful for the few moments alone, even if she was tied up and forced to sit on the floor.

As she sat there her thoughts went to Long Trail Ranch and her parents. Would she ever see them again? Would they ever forgive her? Could she ever forgive herself? What were they doing right now?

Julia thought of the last meal she had had with her parents. Maria had fried chicken and served it with mashed potatoes, gravy, English peas, and biscuits. And, she had made an apple pie, just for Julia.

The thought of the apple pie was too much. The tears she had tried to hold back came streaming down her face.

Kincaid and the others came back into the cabin, still very excited about what they had just done. Julia knew that they had gone to rob a bank, and from their reactions, they must have done just that.

"Ha! Did you see the expression on that old woman's face when we shot her husband?" Hoy asked.

"How do we know he was her husband?" Liddell asked. "Who knows, those two old fogies might've been living in sin."

The others laughed at Liddell's suggestion.

"Yeah, well, they ain't livin' in sin no more, 'cause the old man is gone," Chiles said. "You know what, we might have just saved that old woman's soul."

Now the others laughed uproariously at Chiles' comment.

Julia sat there, horror struck as she listened to their conversation. Apparently, the bank robbery had been successful, but they were actually talking about, no, bragging about, the people they had killed.

She was particularly appalled when they told about a woman they had killed in the bank.

"King brought his pistol down on that old woman's head, then he said to the teller, 'There ain't nobody in front of me now'. Did ya'll see her head? He busted it plumb open," Chiles said to the others.

How could anyone be as cruel as these men?

And how could anyone be as dumb as she was? "Oh, Papa," she said under her breath. "Why didn't I listen to you?"

"You boys stick with me," King said in a loud and authoritative voice. "We'll do a few more jobs, sell this girl back to her pappy and we'll have enough money that we won't have to do nothin' more for the rest of our lives."

"A whore house," Chiles said.

"What?" Hoy asked.

"I'm goin' to go some'ers where they ain't nobody that's never even heard of me, 'n I'm goin' to open me a whore house."

"You'll have to get a woman to run it," Hoy said. "I ain't never been to no whore house what was run by a man."

"I didn't say I was goin' to run it. I'm just goin' to own it. 'N that way all the girls will have to give me a free poke anytime I want one, 'cause if they don't, they'll be out on their asses."

Again, there was loud, raucous laughter.

Julia's cheeks burned red out of the embarrassment of listening to such an open conversation about prostitutes. She knew what a prostitute was and she was beginning to gather some idea of what they did.

"Hey, you know who could be my first whore?" Chiles said. "Iffen her ole' man don't pay to buy her back, I'll buy this little girl we got here, 'n make her my number one whore."

"Yeah? And just who do you plan on buyin' her from?" Kincaid asked.

"Why, I'll buy her from all of you," Chiles said, really beginning to get into the notion now.

"What do you mean you'll buy her from all of us?" Kincaid said.

Julia felt a little twinge of happiness. Jamie was going to protect her after all.

"I'm the one that brung her," Jamie said. "I'm the one you'll buy her from. 'N if Abernathy, that old fool, don't pay the ransom, when all of you get your poke, you'll pay me for it, just like you was in a whore house."

"That ain't right," Liddell said. "King already said we'd cut cards for her."

"You'll be cutting cards for who goes first, but you'll be paying me."

"King, you hearin' this?" Murray asked.

"Kincaid is right," King said. "If we don't ransom her back to the general, the girl's Kincaid's to do whatever he wants with her."

Julia had cried so much that it hurt her throat to cry anymore. That didn't stop the tears though. And as much as she hated Jamie Kincaid now, she hated herself even more. If she could figure out how to do it, she would kill herself.

Eagle Spring Way Station

Although it had taken a considerable effort, Fred Bell was able to sit up now. His entire body was sore and now his face was red, black and blue but most of the swelling was going down.

Leah was bathing his face, gently, with a cloth that had been dipped in cold water.

"Did I hear you say you were a furniture maker?" Leah asked, making conversation to try and take his mind off the considerable pain that she knew he must still be experiencing.

"Yes, ma'am, and if you don't take this as braggin' or actually even if you do, I'm a damn good . . . uh, beg your pardon, I'm a *really* good furniture maker. Why, one of the cabinets I made sits in the mansion of the Missouri governor. When Sterling Price was governor, he bought it."

"Then I don't understand," Leah said.

"What is it you don't understand?"

"If you are that talented of a furniture maker and I've no reason to doubt that you are, why are you . . . .?" She left the question incomplete.

"What am I doing riding the outlaw trail?" Fred replied, completing Leah's question. "The truth is, I've been asking myself that same question since all this started. And the only thing I can say is, I was a fool, as big a fool as you have ever seen. Missouri was a divided state during the war and a lot of us who chose to fight for the South didn't have anything to come back to after the war was over. I had a small furniture shop but the government took it away from me. For taxes, they said, but I have no doubt but that it was because I fought for the South."

"Do you have a family anywhere?"

"My mom and pop are both dead and seeing as how my brother fought for the North and me for the South, well, I guess we never quite worked it out between us. I've had a few jobs here 'n there, but none of them paid very much."

Fred was quiet for a moment. "But I wish now I was still working in Shy's Livery Stable back in Springfield, Missouri."

"Do you like to work with horses then?" Leah asked.

"Yeah. I don't know which I like better, workin' with horses or workin' with wood."

Just then Leah heard the whistle of the incoming train.

"I'd better get out there and see if Papa needs me or if anyone wants some of my bread," Leah said.

Leah had just grabbed her basket and had come out with her father to welcome the train. She saw Will and Gid stepping down from one of the passenger cars, and handing her basket to her father, she ran to meet them.

"Will! Gid!" She called, "You're back!"

"We're back," Gid said in a non-expressive voice.

"You . . . you didn't find Julia, did you?"

Will shook his head. "I'm afraid not," he said, disappointment obvious in his voice.

"What are you going to do now?"

"Colonel Abernathy wants us to keep looking for her

and I expect we will, but it's going to take a little time to figure out what our next move should be."

"How's Fred doing?" Gid asked. "He hasn't run off yet, has he?"

"Now why would you say such a thing? He's been nothing but a gentleman the whole time he's been here."

When Will and Gid went inside, they saw Fred sitting at the table.

"Well, I see you're out of bed," Gid said, "but your face sure looks rough."

"Well, I am feelin' some better. Did you find the little Abernathy girl?" Fred asked.

Will shook his head. "I don't believe Julia's in El Paso. But we did find something interesting there."

"What's that?" Leah asked.

"We found Jamie Kincaid's wife. He married her, took the five hundred dollars she brought to the marriage, then left. No divorce, so technically, he's still married to her."

"That's one sorry son of a . . ." Fred started, but he stopped in mid-sentence. "Sorry Leah."

"You don't have to apologize, Fred," Leah replied. "From what I have heard about him, he is one sorry son of a bitch."

The others laughed.

"How about you, Fred? Do you think you can travel?" Will asked.

Fred sighed. "If you are asking me if I'm recovered enough for you to take me in to the jail, I suppose I am."

"Not so fast, Will," Leah said. "I think he needs several more days before he's fully recovered. You can't take him before a judge with his face looking like it is. Who knows what people might think?"

"I see," Will said. "Let me ask you this, Fred. If that train hold up had been successful, and if you had gotten a couple thousand dollars out of it, would you have left the outlaw trail?"

"Yes, absolutely. All I needed was just . . ." Fred paused. "Actually, Will, the truth is, I don't really know. I told myself that was all I wanted, but I'm not sure they would have let me go after one job. And to be honest, I'm not sure I could have walked away."

"I respect your honesty," Will said.

"I just hope the law does when it comes time for you to turn me in."

Leah reached out to lay her hand on Fred's arm. "I . . . let's talk about something else. I don't want to think about you going to prison."

Shortly after lunch, the telegraph machine began clicking again, and this time it was Buck who hurried over to it. After a few taps of acknowledgement, Buck began receiving and recording the message.

As Buck worked the incoming message, the others continued to visit. When Buck rejoined them a moment later, everyone was laughing at something Gid had said, but the expression on Buck's face stopped everyone in mid-laugh.

"Papa, what is it?" Leah asked. "What's wrong?"

Buck held up the piece of paper he had used to record the incoming telegraph message.

"It seems that the Silas King gang just robbed a bank in Commerce. They got away with several thousand dollars and they killed eight people; one of the ones they killed was a woman."

"Oh, my God, I'm glad I wasn't with them." Fred Bell's almost reverent declaration filled the, otherwise, stunned silence of the room.

"They killed a woman?" Leah asked.

Buck held out the telegram. "That's what it says here. She was a customer in the bank."

"How do they know it was Silas King?" Will asked.

"According to this message, a bar girl heard all the shooting and stepped up to the window to see what was going on. She recognized King."

"We should have killed that son of a bitch back in Lawrence when we had the chance," Gid said. "And I have to confess I did think about it."

"You're wanting to go after King, aren't you?" Fred asked. "I can tell by the look on your face. It's the same look you got when a damn Yankee did something really wrong."

"You've read me right, Fred. I do want to go after him. Gid, are you up to a little raid? I say that the two of us go back to that little encampment and raise some hell. I'm damn sure they won't be expecting us."

"They won't be there," Fred said.

"What do you mean, they won't be there?"

"That's not their regular hiding place. We were just there because we were about to hold up the train. You saw how they all pulled out once they finished beatin' on me."

"Do you know where they are?" Will asked.

"Well sir, I know where their regular hiding place is. I can't promise you they'll be there, but that's where I'd think they would be."

"Where is it?"

"It's on Devils River in Cascade Canyon. I know they have an old abandoned cabin there and that's where they've been staying."

Will turned to Buck Godfrey.

"Mr. Godfrey, I wonder if we might leave Fred here with you for a while," Will asked.

"How long is a while and why would you want to leave him with us?"

"I can't tell you how long it will be because I don't know. But I want to get Silas King, not only for what he did to Fred and was about to do to Gid and me, but also for what he just did over in Commerce. I haven't seen any new posters on King, but seeing as how he just escaped, I would bet there is a reward out for him."

"That's a bet you would win quite easily," Buck said. "Let me show you something."

Will and Gid followed Buck over to the table, whereupon set the telegraph key and a rather large, cubby cabinet.

"I recall getting a telegraph message about King just a few weeks or so ago. It also listed all the members of his gang and I know I've got it. Just give me a moment."

Rifling through the papers in the cubby holes, Buck finally came up with what he was looking for.

"Here it is," he said, then he began reading. "Silas King, prison escapee, one thousand dollars, Kit Chiles, prison escapee seven-hundred-and-fifty dollars. And there is a two hundred dollar reward for each of the rest of his gang: Perry Hoy, Val Baker, Abe Haller, Andy Murray, Frog Jones, Spider Liddell, and Sly Aikens. Of course, Halley and Aikens are dead and the rewards have been paid." Buck looked toward Fred. "Your name isn't on here, son."

"No, sir, I don't reckon it would be since I only just joined up with 'em."

"As for leaving Fred here with us for a while, I feel no sense of danger from him," Buck said. "What about you, Leah? Does it make you nervous?"

"No, Papa, it doesn't make me nervous in the slightest,"

Leah said as she reached over to pat Fred's hand.

Buck looked over toward Will and Gid. "I know you boys said you wanted to get after Silas King, but how are you going to do that when you came in here on foot dragging Fred behind you?"

"Damn," Will said. "We'll have to go to Jericho before we can start out. We'll have to buy a couple of mounts."

"I can take care of that for you," Leah said.

"You?" Gid questioned, surprised by the announcement.

"Leah raises horses," Buck said with a proud smile. "She has some of the best horseflesh you will ever see anywhere."

"I suppose you'll need saddles as well," Leah said.

"Yes."

"You'll also need a couple of long guns," Buck said.

"That would be good, since we lost our rifles with our saddles."

"I sell rifles and ammunition," Buck said. "I don't do a booming business, but I sell enough to keep me doing it. How about a couple of Henrys? Would that do you?"

"Yes, sir, that would do us fine indeed," Will replied. "It might strain us a bit to pay for them, but I wouldn't want to go against King and his gang without a rifle."

"You don't need to buy 'em, just bring 'em back when you're through with 'em," Buck said with an accommodating smile. "If you find King, you might just recover your guns and your horses."

"Well, Mr. Godfrey, we thank you for that," Gid said.

"Come along with me," Leah said. "The horses are out back and I'll let you pick out whichever ones you think you would like to ride."

Will and Gid followed Leah out through the back of the way station and down a small path to a barn and corral they hadn't noticed before.

"We built the barn and stable here behind this little bluff in order to give the horses some protection against the weather," Leah said.

"Oh, my these are good looking horses," Gid said as the eight animals came trotting over to the corral fence to greet them. "You do know your horse flesh, Leah."

"Yes, I do, thank you. Now you can see why I admired your two horses," Leah said. She pointed to two of the horses who stood apart from the other eight. "Those two belonged to the outlaws you killed during the train robbery. These six are the ones I've been raising."

"You said we could pick out whichever ones we wanted. Do you have any suggestions?"

"What about these two?" Leah suggested, as she pointed to two of them. "This is Prince and that's Dandy."

Prince and Dandy came over to put their muzzles in Leah's hand and she lay her face up against them and spoke to them.

"Wow, they really care for you," Gid said.

"That's because they know I love them."

"Well, thank you for trusting us with them," Will said.

With the two horses saddled, Will and Gid returned to the way station. When they went inside, Buck had two Henry rifles on the counter, with two boxes of .44 cartridges by each rifle.

"You've got a hundred rounds apiece," Buck said.

"How much do we owe you for this?"

"Like I said earlier, for the rifles, nothing, if you bring them back in good condition. But when you've got money again, I'll charge you fifty cents a box for the bullets."

Half an hour later, mounted on Prince and Dandy, as fine a pair of horses as Will and Gid had ever ridden, the two brothers started toward the Devils Mountains.

Cascade Canyon The outlaw hideout

At the outlaw's cabin, the gang was still talking about the bank robbery they had so recently conducted.

"Whooee," Baker said with a laugh. "Did you ever see a prettier explosion? Them boys got blowed all to hell when that bridge went up."

"I'll tell you what I liked," Chiles said. "I liked the expression on the face of that old son of a bitch that was loadin' the buckboard when I shot 'im."

"We didn't get none of us kilt, or hurt, or nothin',"

Liddell said. "This here was most the best job we ever have done."

"How about the money?" Hoy asked. "When are we goin' to split up the money? We've had it for four days now."

"Yeah, I'd like to get my hands on some of that money too," Baker said.

"All right, I'll divide it up right now," King said.

King took the money from the sack, then began counting it out into eleven equal piles.

"Hey, they's only ten of us," Murray said. "What for are you countin' it out into eleven shares?"

"One share goes to Kincaid, 'n I'm takin' two shares for myself." King replied. He fixed an evil stare upon Murray. "You'll be gettin' close to nine hunnert dollars apiece. You got 'ny questions about that?"

"No," Murray acquiesced quickly. "I ain't got no questions, I mean, you bein' the boss 'n all, it's only fittin' that you should get an extra share."

"Hey, King, after we get the money all divided up, you got 'ny objections to some of us goin' over to Caliham 'n gettin' us a couple of drinks, 'n maybe a woman to poke?"

"I don't care, but don't go gettin' wild in town just yet. All you'll do is start folks to wonderin' how it is that you've come by so much money, 'n it bein' so soon after the Commerce job, they might get to figurein' out where it come from. 'N don't get drunk. If you get drunk 'n get a woman, next thing you know you're goin' to start braggin', 'n you'll be a sayin' somethin' you shouldn't."

"Well, hell, what if we just took thirty dollars with us? That ain't all that much, 'n lots of times cowboys will ride into town 'n spend ever' thing they was just paid."

King didn't answer right away. Instead he just did a quick recount of the eleven stacks of money he had laid on the table before him, then with a smile, he took two of the stacks for himself.

"All right, you can go," he said. "But just remember what I told you about spendin' so much that someone is liable to get curious."

"Come on, Frog, Andy," Spider Murray said to Baker and Jones. "I know they's a woman in Caliham that's wantin' me so bad that hell, she's liable to pay me for a poke."

Frog Jones laughed. "Spider, you're as full of shit as a Christmas turkey."

At the moment, Will and Gid were six miles east of the outlaw cabin, having followed Devils River as Fred had told them to do.

"I tell you what, Little Brother. I think that once we get into Cascade Canyon itself, it might be that we'll want to back off from the river a bit," Will suggested.

"How are we goin' to do that? The river runs right through the middle of the canyon," Gid replied.

"We'll trail along up top, on the canyon ridge."

"Damn, I knew you were going to say that," Gid replied.

Will chuckled. "Then why did you ask?"

"Because I was kind of hoping you wouldn't say that."

"You got any other way of finding the cabin without being seen?" Will asked.

"No," Gid replied without any particular enthusiasm.

They weren't sure how the horses would take the climb up to the top of the ridge line, but they did so with comparative ease. Once they were on top, every fifteen minutes or so they would stop and Will would step out to the edge to see if they had gone past the cabin Fred had told them about. Will was the one who had to check, because Gid couldn't force himself to stand out on the lip of the canyon.

Eagle Spring Way Station

"What did you say this was?" Fred asked, as he examined the drink Leah had just given him.

"It's called a mint julep," Leah replied. "Are you saying you've never had one?"

"No ma'am, the only thing I've ever drunk is whiskey and beer mostly, oh, and some wine."

"Well, then it's about time you tried something new, isn't it?"

"And you're supposed to drink it out of a silver cup?"

Fred asked, lifting the cup.

"That's what tradition says," Leah said. She held her cup out toward Fred. "Take a sip," she invited.

With a curious expression on his face, Fred lifted the cup to his lips and took a swallow. The curious expression was replaced with a broad smile.

"Whoo wee, this is one good tasting drink," he said.

"I thought you might like it."

"Where did you learn to make something like this?"

"Papa taught me," Leah said. Leah got a serious expression on her face. "Fred, do you think you'll go to prison?"

Fred nodded. "Yes, ma'am, I expect I will."

"Have you ever been in prison?"

"No, I've never been in any proper prison but I have been in jail a few times." He smiled. "Mostly it was for getting drunk, but I've never gotten drunk on anything like this. Can you get drunk on . . . what did you call it, a mint julep?"

"A mint julep, yes, and I'm sure you could get drunk if you drank enough of them, but the proper etiquette is to have no more than one drink at a time, and you can't get drunk on just one drink."

"No, it sure doesn't seem like you could."

"Do you think the Crockett Brothers will take you to prison?"

"I don't know, that's where we were headed when some

of King's men hit us. So, I reckon they will."

"I thought they were friends of yours," Leah said. "And after you saved their lives."

"Well, I've been thinking about it," Fred said. "If they hadn't shot me when they did, I would have most likely stayed with King, and if I had been with him in this bank robbery in Commerce, I might well have killed someone. Then if they caught me it wouldn't have been just jail; I would more 'n likely be hanged."

"Would you really have killed someone?" Leah asked. "I mean if you had been in that bank robbery."

"I don't know," Fred said. "I killed some people during the war, but they were trying to kill me. But I haven't killed anyone since the war. As I sit here right now, I tell you I wouldn't want to kill anybody, but I suppose if I was put in a place where I'd have to do it, why I expect I'd kill again."

Leah took another sip of her mint julep, then was quiet for a long moment.

"I don't want you to go to prison, Fred."

"I . . . I don't want to go. But it would be better to go and get it over with, than it would be, to be a wanted man and have the law and bounty hunters coming after you."

"I suppose there is some truth to that," Leah admitted.

"Besides, if Will and Gid are the ones who take me in, I know they'll speak well of me, so I most likely won't have to be in prison for very long at all."

Chapter Seventeen

"I'm goin' into Caliham to have a look around," King said. "That's another town like Commerce; it's got a fat little bank and very little law. I figure if we hit that one, we'll have enough money to divide up 'n go most anywhere we'd like."

"What about the girl?" Chiles asked.

"What about her?"

"Well, ain't we goin' to get some money from her pappy for givin' her back to 'em? I mean if Kincaid got a share of the money we got from robbin' the bank, don't the rest of us get a share from sellin' the girl back to her Papa?"

"Anybody as is still here then will get a share. But once we hit the bank in Caliham, like I said, we'd have enough money to go anywhere we might want, even without waitin' on the money for the girl."

"Where would you go, King?" Chiles asked.

"Missouri."

"Missouri, really?" Chiles laughed. "Now why in hell would you want to go to Missouri?"

"I come from Missouri. My pa was a sharecropper 'n I worked on the farm with him. We was dirt poor, 'n the folks in Mississippi County didn't treat us poor whites no different from the slaves. I intend to go back to Missouri with enough money to tell everyone there to kiss my ass."

The others laughed.

"But first, I'll be goin' into Caliham."

"If you're goin' into Caliham, how long will you be gone?" Hoy asked.

"No more 'n a day or two."

"Reason I asked, is do you have any problem with some us goin' into Tierra Malvada?"

"Don't all of you go at the same time. And be careful," King warned.

"What about you, Kincaid? You want to go into town with us? You ain't been out of this camp in a coon's age."

"The girl? Have you thought about her?" Kincaid asked.

"Hell, I'll stay with Julia," Murray said, looking at the young girl with lust-filled eyes.

When Julia heard her name mentioned, she began paying closer attention to the conversation. Would Jamie actually leave her here? Jamie was the one who brought her here in the first place, so she had no reason to feel safer with him than she would with any of the others, but she would rather be with the devil she knew, than the devil she didn't know.

"Jamie don't leave me here," Julia said in a frightened voice.

"Murray, if you do stay with her, don't you do nothin' to her yet," King said. "If we sell her back to her pa, we'll get more money if we ain't touched her. Besides, if we do decide to have our fun with 'er, we'll be doin' it like I said we was. We'll cut high card to who goes first."

"First after me," Kincaid said.

King looked at the girl. "Makes you almost hope her pappy won't want 'er back."

Kincaid, Chiles, Baker and Hoy left the cabin, with only King and Murray staying behind.

"I'm warnin' you, Murray," King said.

"Yeah, yeah, I know, I ain't goin' to do nothin' to her."

"Because if you do, I'll kill you," King added.

Soon after the four men had ridden out, Will and Gid, were on the lip of the canyon wall, looking down onto the cabin.

"So, what do we do next? Send some boulders crashing down on it?" Gid teased.

"Not that bad of an idea if we could . . . wait a minute, something's happening."

"Is that who we think it is?" Gid asked.

"I do believe it is, Little Brother! Our quarry's in sight."

"It looks to me like King's leaving," Gid said as they watched him saddle his horse. "I wonder where he's going."

"I don't know and I don't care, as long as we can get ahead of him," Will said.

"What'll we do if we can't?" Gid asked.

"We'll lose a thousand dollars," Will replied with a broad grin.

"Look's like he's headin' east. Come on."

King had been considering his possibilities and that was when he had come up with the idea of robbing the bank in Caliham. He told the others he was going to scout it out and he was. But his real intention was to see if he could rob the bank himself; he wouldn't share the money with anyone.

That would leave the business with the girl unfinished, but he would let the others deal with that. Whether they actually tried to get money from her pa, or whether they took their turns with her, it wouldn't make any difference to him, he'd be on his way to Missouri.

He knew that the Crocketts could come back to cause him a problem. He remembered them as being fierce warriors, though not as willing to kill as he was. If that son of a bitch Fred Bell hadn't let them go, they'd be dead by now.

But Bell . . . King concluded, with a little chuckle. He'd taken care of him, or at least the critters had.

When the Crockett brothers dropped back down onto the Devils River trail, they knew they were ahead of King and they knew he would have to come this way, because there was no other way he could go.

They heard the sound off the hoof beats growing louder until they knew that he was right upon them. With guns drawn, they moved out to block him.

"What the hell?" King shouted, as his horse reared up in surprise. After he got the horse under control, he made a grab for his pistol but Will's shot carried his hat away and frightened, he jerked his hand away from the pistol.

"Don't shoot, don't shoot! I ain't a' drawin', I ain't goin' for my gun."

"King, you know that shot could easily have been your head," Will said, holding the smoking gun.

"What do you want?" King asked. "Money?"

"We don't want anything; we've got you," Will said.

"What the hell do you want with me? You ain't the law."

"No we're not, but we can sure as hell turn you over to the law and then collect your bounty," Gid said.

"Bounty? You mean to tell me you are a couple of damn bounty hunters?" King asked. "How much is the bounty on me?"

"Last we heard, it was a thousand dollars, but I expect it went up after you robbed the bank in Commerce," Gid said. "Tell me, why did you have to kill so many?"

"Don't tell me there ain't neither one of you what's never killed anybody," King said. "You can't 'cause I seen it with my own eyes, remember that Yankee pay officer? He had four men with him and you two took out ever' one of 'em."

"That was different, and you know it," Will said. "It was war."

"What about this?" King offered. "Let's say that, for old time's sake, I give you boys five thousand dollars in cash and we each go on our merry ways? Even if they is a bounty on me, it ain't likely to be that much"

"No deal," Will said, resolutely. He took out a rope, opened the noose, then dropped it over King's head.

"Look here, what are you a doin'?" King asked, the sound of his voice reflecting his fear. "You . . . you ain't plannin' on hangin' me, are you?"

"I've given it some thought," Will said, as he tightened the noose. Will looked over at Gid and nodded. That was the signal for his brother to loop his rope around King's neck as well.

"What is this? What are you a doin'?"

"We're taking you into Jericho and turning you over to the sheriff," Will said.

"Well, you can't have these ropes around my neck," King complained. "What if my horse was to suddenly decide to bolt off?"

"That would probably break your neck. Or else strangle you. Either way, you'd be dead," Will said. "Having our ropes around you like this will make certain that we can get you into town."

"This ain't right. I mean, we're old friends, hell we fought 'n the war together."

"Yeah, you showed us what friends we were when you tied us to a tree," Gid said.

"I didn't actual do nothin' to you though, did I? Hell, I was tryin' to scare you a bit. I was plannin' on lettin' you go the next mornin'."

"Oh yeah, I'm sure that was your plan," Will said sarcastically. "But we aren't going to let you go, so if I were you, I'd make sure my horse didn't suddenly decide to run off."

Eagle Spring

"Chocolate cake?" Fred said with a broad smile. "You made a chocolate cake?"

"For your birthday," Leah said.

"But this isn't my birthday. My birthday's in November."

"Did you get a cake for your birthday?" Leah asked

with a teasing smile.

"No. Actually I can't even remember the last time I had a cake."

"Well, you have one now," Leah said. "That is, unless you don't want it."

"Oh, no, I want it! I reckon that right now, I want it just about more than anything you could think about."

"Then what if we both have a piece of this cake and a cup of coffee?" Leah offered.

She cut the cake, then came over to help Fred get from the bed to the table.

Fred held up his hand. "I think I can do it myself. Anyway, I'd like to try."

Leah stood beside him. "I'm here if you need me," she said as the two of them walked slowly, from the bed where Fred had been recuperating, to the table.

Fred made it, and with a triumphant smile, he sat down.

"There, you did that very well," Leah said. She picked up the coffee pot and held it just over Fred's cup.

"Do you take cream or sugar?" she asked.

"Just black," Fred replied.

Fred watched as Leah poured coffee into the two cups, then added cream and sugar to her own. She stirred her coffee until it became a light brown.

"This is nice," Fred said, "the two of us, eating cake

and drinking coffee. Why, it's almost like one of those box lunch socials where the man has to buy the lunch in order to sit with the girl. Except this time, I didn't have to buy anything."

"You didn't have to buy a box lunch, but I do want you to pay for it," Leah said.

"Yes, ma'am, I'll be glad to pay for it. But the problem is, I don't have any money right now."

Leah chuckled, then reached across the table to lay her hand on his. He felt an unexpected charge of excitement from the touch.

"I don't want any money," she said. "But Papa has some lumber and some tin out in the machine shed. I wonder if you could build me a kitchen cupboard. I'll be glad to pay you for it."

"Leah, I'll build you the prettiest kitchen cupboard you've ever seen," Fred promised.

Chapter Eighteen

Red Garter Saloon – Jericho

Minnie didn't have a last name, which was all right because her name wasn't Minnie, either. Her real name was Alice Woods and she had left her family in Memphis when she was seventeen years old. She was twenty-four now and though she was still a pretty girl, the dissipation of her profession was beginning to show, despite the artifice of rouge and paint.

At the moment, Minnie was standing at the bar, staring morosely into her drink. Unlike the drinks the customers normally bought her, this drink was real whisky and not tea.

"Minnie, are you all right?" Clint Weatherby asked. Clint, who was the bartender, made several swipes of the bar in front of her.

"It's my fault," Minnie said. "I was a fool to think that any man could ever love a woman like me."

"No, Harry Slater is the fool," Clint said. "You're a fine woman, Minnie, as fine a woman as any I've ever met. And trust me, you're better off without him."

Minnie smiled. "You know what? You're right. Nobody forced me into this life; I made my own choice to do this. I'm going to find some lonely cowboy and cheer him up and it'll cheer me up, too." She saw a new customer come into the saloon and she smiled, and started toward him.

Yeah, Val Baker thought when he saw a bar girl coming toward him. He had thirty dollars in his pocket and this was why he had come to town. The others had gone to Tierra Malvada, but he had decided he'd rather be on his own, so he had come to Jericho.

"Hello, cowboy, my name's Minnie. Would you like some company?"

"That's what I'm here for and I've got money to spend," Baker said.

The arrival in town of the Crocketts and Silas King caught the attention of all. And why shouldn't it? It wasn't every day that one would see a man riding into town with two nooses around his neck.

"Hey, you know who that is?" someone said. "That

feller's Silas King."

"Who?"

"Silas King, the murderer."

"Son of a bitch, what's he doin' in Jericho?"

The first man laughed. "I don't know, but it looks to me like he didn't come here of his own free will. I expect he's a' goin' to jail."

Win and Gid led a sullen Silas King down to the jail.

"I'd suggest you'd better get down from that horse real easy," Will said. "We wouldn't want anything to happen to you."

Once the three men were dismounted, they went into the sheriff's office, where they saw a man, wearing a star, sitting behind a desk.

"Are you the sheriff?" Will asked.

"Yes, Patrick O'Shea, what can I do for . . ." Sheriff O'Shea stopped in mid-sentence and stared at one of the men. He lifted his finger and pointed at the man in the middle.

"Is that Silas King?" the sheriff asked.

"You don't have to talk like I ain't here, you bald-headed son a bitch. Just ask me."

"Are you Silas King?"

"Yeah, but don't you be a' startin' no necktie parties just yet."

200

"Bring him back here," Sheriff O'Shea said, leading the way to the back of the jail. "I've got a nice place just waitin' for him."

"Here," Will said, handing the sheriff an envelope."

"What's that?"

"It's a little over seventeen hundred dollars we found in his saddle bag. I imagine it came from the bank in Commerce."

"Well," Sheriff O'Shea said. "I congratulate you boys on your honesty. You could've kept that money and no one would have been the wiser."

"Will you be able to authorize the reward payment?" Will asked when the sheriff returned from having locked up King.

"Let me send a telegram to Austin. I can probably have authorization for payment by tomorrow and for sure, no later than the next day."

"How much is the reward?" Gid asked.

"It's been increased since the bank robbery in Commerce." Sheriff O'Shea smiled. "Now it's twenty-five hundred dollars."

"We'll be down at the Red Garter if you hear anything," Will said.

Leaving the sheriff's office, the two brothers, with a bounce in their step over the amount of the reward, walked down the street to the saloon. When they went inside, they stepped up to the bar and ordered a beer.

"Hey, Clint, them's the two men what brung Silas King in," one of the patrons of the saloon called out. "I seen 'em just a'fore I come in here. They come a' ridin' in here bigger 'n life, with them ropes around King's neck."

"Is that true?" the bartender asked as he set the beers on the counter.

"It is," Will said as he put a dime on the bar for the two beers.

The bartender pushed the dime back. "No sir, you won't be payin' for your drinks for as long as you're in my bar. Anyone who brought that murdering son of bitch in can have anything he wants in here for free."

"Uh, does that include supper?" Gid asked.

"Sure, if you're all right with ham and fried taters," Clint said. "That's all we got."

"Ham and fried potatoes sounds like just the meal I want," Gid said.

"And you?" Clint asked Will.

Will smiled. "Sounds good to me as well."

Val Baker and Minnie came down the stairs then and Minnie went immediately out onto the floor to move among the men with a practiced smile. Baker stepped up to the bar for a drink.

"I didn't think anybody'd ever capture King again," a

customer standing at the bar said to the man next to him. "Did you read 'bout what happened over in Commerce? They robbed the bank, 'n killt themselves five people. One of 'em they killt was the school marm who just happened to be in the bank when they was robbin' it."

"I heard it was seven they kilt. When they hang that murderin' son of a bitch, I plan to be in the front row," the other customer said.

"Where is King now?" Baker asked, turning to the man beside him.

"Why, I expects he's right here in our jail," one of the men replied with a big smile. "Yes, sir, when it comes time to hang the son of a bitch, we'll be the ones that's doin' it, seein' as we're the ones that captured 'im."

"Now, Paul, that ain't quite true," the bartender said. "Them two eatin' at that table over there's the ones that brought 'em in."

When Baker looked toward the table he recognized them as the two men they had held captured for a while until Bell let them go. Then, he had a feeling of apprehension. If he recognized them, they could certainly recognize him.

Baker let himself out the back door as if he were going to the toilet. Then, he hurried around the outside of the building back up to the street where he mounted his horse and rode away. He had to tell the others about this.

Eagle Spring

Fred and Leah walked out to the machine shed together. "Now, stop right here," Fred said. "I need to put my hands over your eyes so that you can't see 'till I'm ready for you to see."

Stepping up behind her, Fred put his hands over her eyes. She reached up and put her hand over his, squeezing it slightly and again, he felt a strange surging feeling.

"Don't let me fall," Leah said.

"Don't worry, I won't let you fall," Fred said.

"I'd feel better if your hands were on my waist. I'll cover my own eyes."

"All right," Fred said. Standing behind her, with his hands on her waist, he noticed that his breathing had become quicker and shallower.

They started into the shed and Leah, as if to improve her balance, leaned back against him.

"All right," Fred said. "You can take your hands away from your eyes now."

"Does that mean you have to take your hands off me?" Leah asked.

"What?" Fred's response was practically a gasp.

"Never mind," Leah said, with a little laugh. "I'm teasing you."

"Here it is," Fred said, extending his hand toward the cupboard.

The cupboard was four feet tall and almost as wide. It had two drawers at the top and two paneled doors on the bottom. Fred had even carved wooden knobs that looked like horse heads. He had sanded the wood until it shone with a rich patina.

"Oh!" Leah said. "Oh, I have never seen anything so beautiful! Fred. I'll be so proud to have that in our kitchen and I'm so proud of you for crafting it."

As part of Leah's enthusiasm, she gave him a light kiss on the lips, but the kiss quickly deepened by mutual accord. Leah wasn't prepared for her reaction to the kiss, her head began to spin and she felt a tingling throughout her whole body. The kiss lasted but a few seconds and yet, even when their lips separated, the wobbly feeling in her body continued.

"I," she started. "I think maybe we should go inside," she said.

"Leah, I'm sorry. I didn't mean to take advantage of you and . . ."

Leah's chuckle was short and self-deprecating. "What makes you think you were the one taking advantage?"

Outlaw Cabin

It was two days before all the men returned from their "excursions" into town, and that was when Baker told them about King being held in the Jericho jail.

"We need to bust him out of there," Baker said.

"Bust him out? What the hell for?" Hoy asked.

"Well, for one thing, he busted me out of prison," Chiles said.

"Yeah, 'n for another thing, he's the one what planned the bank robbery that got us the money we got now," Hoy said.

After some discussion, they decided they would rescue their leader.

Will and Gid had been three days in Jericho waiting for the transfer of funds to pay them their reward. They were in the Red Garter when Sheriff O'Shea came in with a broad smile.

"Here you go, boys, I expect this is what you two been waitin' around for." He put two thousand five hundred dollars down on their table. "I'll let you two figure out how to divide it up," he added with a chuckle.

"Thanks Sheriff," Will said.

Sheriff O'Shea stretched. "Well, I reckon I had better get home to the little woman," he said. "She don't like it all that much when I'm late gettin' home, but when I got word that your reward had been authorized, I wanted to bring it to you myself."

"King's doing all right, is he?" Gid asked.

"Well, he don't like bein' in jail, but that's where he's goin' to stay until his trial. Deputy Lopez is on duty tonight, he'll keep a good watch on him. We can count on that."

"Where to next?" Gid asked after the sheriff left.

"I don't know. I'm sort of dumbfounded right now. Julia can't have just disappeared, but I sure don't know where to go next," Will said.

"Do you ever wonder if we're doing the right thing?" Gid asked.

"What do you mean?"

"Julia ran away with Kincaid; he didn't kidnap her. She left with him because she wanted to. What if we are just interfering with two people who are in love?"

"You do remember Polly, don't you? Jamie Kincaid's wife?"

"Oh, yeah," Gid said. "I hadn't thought about that. So, where do we go now? You don't think Julia is dead, do you?"

"I hope not, but the longer it takes us to find her, the more likely that is, unless it's like you said, that she's as happy as a pig in shit, but for tonight I intend to get me a good night's sleep."

Chapter Nineteen

The town of Jericho, which buzzed with commerce by day, and rang with joyous pleasure seekers by night had, by two o'clock in the morning, finally grown quiet. Chiles, Baker, Hoy, Jones, Liddell and Murray walked their horses quietly into town, then headed for the jail house which was at the far end of Front Street. Hoy was leading a saddled, but riderless horse.

From somewhere in the town they heard a baby crying, followed by a barking dog. A freshening breeze caught one of the signs and as it swung back and forth the chain rattled.

When they reached the jail house, Chiles signaled for Hoy and Murray to stay with the horses, while the rest of them went into the jail, still moving as quietly as possible.

There was a jailer sitting behind a desk, his hands clasped together across his stomach, and he was snoring loudly.

"Hell, ain't no need to be too quiet," Jones said. "A train could come through here 'n it wouldn't wake up that son of a bitch."

Deputy Lopez who had been asleep, suddenly woke up to see four men standing in front of the desk, pointing their pistols at him.

"What? What is this?" Lopez asked.

Chiles cocked his pistol. "Be quiet," he ordered.

Lopez's eyes opened wide in fear and he began to tremble.

"Stay here with him," Chiles said. "I'm going to talk to Silas."

King had been asleep when the men came in, but was awakened by their encounter with the jailer and now he stood with his hands wrapped around the bars of his cell. Frightened at first that it may have been a lynch mob, he smiled in relief when he saw Chiles.

"Good man!"

Chiles smiled. "You got me out of prison, so I figure I owe you."

Chiles walked back out to the front. "Where's the key?" he asked Lopez.

"I can't tell you that."

Chiles cocked the pistol then pointed it at Lopez's head. "It don't look to me like you got much choice. You'll either tell us, or we'll kill you and find the damn key ourselves."

With shaking hands, Lopez opened the drawer then pulled out a ring of keys. "It's this one," he said.

"Check it out, Jones."

Jones took the key, went into the back then appeared a moment later with a smiling Silas King.

"Where's my money?" King asked the Deputy.

"The sheriff, he sent the money back to the bank," Lopez said.

"We don't need him anymore," King said, nodding toward the deputy.

With an evil smile on his face, Chiles pulled the trigger and a black hole appeared in Lopez's forehead.

"All right, let's get movin' 'fore somebody comes to see what the shot was all about."

When they cleared the town, King held up his hand to stop them.

"Boys, I got a favor to ask," he said.

"Hell, Silas, we just got you out of jail, what more do you want?" Hoy asked.

"There's someplace we need to stop 'fore we go back to the cabin," King said.

"Where's that? You ain't thinkin' 'bout robbin' no bank,

not at this hour of the mornin'."

"Nope, I wanna go to the Eagle Spring Way Station," King said.

"Whatever for?" Murray asked. "They sure as hell don't have no money at that place and we ain't gonna catch a train."

"I heard the Crocketts talkin' about Fred Bell."

"What about Bell? Didn't we leave that son of a bitch dead in the dirt."

King shook his head. "No, he warn't dead. The Crocketts took 'im back to Eagle Spring, 'n and I 'spect he told 'em where to find the hideout."

"What? You mean they can find the cabin?" Chiles asked.

"Yeah, they grabbed me about a mile away, so's I know they seen it. We have to find someplace else to be, but before we do, I intend to stop by and kill that bastard traitor."

Feeling the urge to urinate, Fred got up in the middle of the night and went outside, choosing to walk as much as a hundred feet away from the house. That was when he saw the riders approaching, appearing out of the darkness.

"If the son of a bitch is here, we'll find him."

Fred recognized that voice. It was the voice of Silas King. How did King even know that he was here?

"Chiles, you 'n Hoy go into the house, light ever' lantern ya find, 'n get everybody out here," King ordered.

Fred had advanced to the well and was now hiding behind it. They had lit torches and in the flickering golden light he could see Leah and Buck when they were brought from the house. Leah was in a sleeping gown, and Buck was in his underwear.

"Where's Fred Bell?" King asked Chiles, who had led the search through the house.

"We didn't see him," Chiles said.

"You," King said to Buck. "Where's Bell?"

"I don't know," Buck answered.

"He's here someplace, least wise his clothes are here," Hoy said.

"You," King said as he grabbed Leah's arm. "Where is that bastard?"

"I don't know," she said.

"Maybe this'll help you remember where he is," Chiles said.

There was the sound of a gunshot and Buck cried out in pain. He had been shot in the knee.

"Papa!" Leah shouted trying to get away from King's grip.

"I'm only going to ask you one more time. Where's Bell?"

"I . . . I don't know," Buck replied in a voice that reflected his pain.

There was another shot and Fred saw Buck go down with a bullet to his other knee.

"Where is the son of a bitch?" King asked again.

"Leave him alone!" Leah said. "Can't you see he doesn't know where Fred is?"

"Then we're wasting our time with him, aren't we?" King said. He pulled the trigger and this time his bullet hit Buck in the center of his chest.

"Papa, no!" Leah screamed at the top of her voice.

"Find Bell," King ordered, as the others spread out going to all corners of the way station.

Fred realized that if they came behind the house, they were sure to see him. And if they did, he had no doubt he would be killed. He didn't think they would kill Leah, but if she needed any kind of help, he would have to stay alive.

Then, on a sudden inspiration, he climbed over the lip of the well and going hand over hand on the windless, he lowered himself to the very bottom where he was able to stand on the narrow ledge of rock that encircled the water. The ledge was so narrow that the footing was precarious and here it was so dark that he couldn't see his hand in front of his face. There was absolutely no way they would be able to see him down here.

He could hear their voices as they called back and forth to one another.

"Looks like there's a barn back there, let's go see."

He could hear other snippets of conversation, understandable if they were close, but not if they were too far away.

"Lookie what I found," Murray said.

"Good. Is it Bell?" King asked.

"No, but ain't these the horses that Aikens and Haller was ridin' when we tried to hold up the train? They was just standin' out there by the fence, waitin' for us to take 'em," Murray said. "I think they knowed it was us."

"They's a waterin' trough over there by the well," Frog said. "Let's give 'em a good drink and get out of here."

Someone pulled the rope on the bucket and Fred made certain it was full of water as it made its way to the top.

"Everbody, fill your canteens while we got easy water," King shouted.

Once again the bucket was lowered and Fred filled the bucket, being careful not to lose his purchase on the ledge. He was glad he was barefooted.

He breathed a sigh of relief as the bucket cleared his head on its way to the top.

"Should we keep searchin' for Bell?" Chiles asked.

"Naw, who knows where the son of a bitch is now," King said, "but did you hear this little missy call him Fred? That means somethin' to me. If we take her with us, it'll be like bees comin' to honey. He'll come after us and then we'll have him right where we want him."

"Who's she goin' to ride double with?" Murray asked.

"Won't need to," someone said. "Throw a saddle on one of them two horses you found, or are you claimin' 'em for your ownself?"

A few minutes later, Fred heard the horses leaving and as far as he could tell, they had not taken Leah's pet horses. Even though he felt a sense of hopelessness knowing they were taking Leah with them, he knew that he could go after her as soon as he got out of the well. At that moment, as improbable as it may seem, he realized that he was in love with Leah Godfrey.

He remained quiet until he was sure no one was still around, then he decided to climb up out of the well.

Except the last time the bucket had been drawn up, no one had sent it back down. He couldn't get out of the well.

"My God," Fred said and it was more of a prayer than an oath. "Am I going to die down here?"

Will and Gid were having breakfast when Sheriff O'Shea came into the cafe and started looking around, anxiously.

"There's O'Shea," Gid said.

"Probably coming to see us off," Will replied.

"I don't think so, Big Brother. Something's happened, I can tell by the expression on his face."

Will checked it out. "I think you're right. Sheriff?" Will

called, just loud enough to get O'Shea's attention.

At Will's call, O'Shea hurried over to the brothers' table. As he got closer, his agitation was even more noticeable.

"He's dead," Sheriff O'Shea said.

"King?"

"No, my deputy, Lopez. He's dead and King's gone."

Outlaw Cabin

When King and the others reached the cabin, they brought a trussed-up Leah with them. That was when she saw another young woman tied and sitting on the floor near the wall.

"Get down there, next to the other one," King said, enforcing his order by pushing Leah to the floor. "Tie 'em together and don't let 'em move."

Chiles got a rope and first, tied Leah's hands together, then wrapped a rope around the two women over and over in a figure eight, ending with tying yet another rope to the leg of the stove.

"Now rustle up some grub," King said. "I ain't had a bite to eat since them bastards took me to jail."

"Who are you?" Julia whispered.

"My name's Leah Godfrey. Who are you?"

"Julia Abernathy."

"You!" Leah said. "You're the one Will and Gid are looking for."

"Will and Gid are looking for me?" Julia replied, her eyes opening wide.

"Yes, they are, but they think you ran away to get married."

"I did," Julia said. "But he . . . ." she choked up as tears began to stream down her face. "He brought me here," she said. "*He's one of them.*"

Julia began crying and Leah wanted to comfort her, but her arms were tied so she couldn't give her an embrace. She did the next best thing and wriggled her body close enough to Julia, that the young girl could rest her head on Leah's shoulder.

Julia wept for some time, and even after she quit crying aloud, Leah could feel the occasional jerking movement of her body. When she had quieted, Julia lifted her head. "I'm so sorry," she said.

"Don't be, you have nothing to apologize for."

"It's just that I have been here for, I really don't know how long. You are the first person I've seen who doesn't want to . . . ."

"You don't have to say it, I understand," Leah said.

"Who are you? Why did they bring you here?"

Leah explained that she worked at the Eagle Spring

Way Station and how King and his men had come in the night and killed her father.

"Oh, Leah," Julia said as she started to cry again.

"No, Julia, don't cry. Under these circumstances, the only thing we can do is be strong and give one another what comfort we can."

Julia smiled. "I'm so sorry you had to go through what has happened to you, but for this minute, this day, I'm glad you're here. When you said the Crocketts are looking for me that gives me hope." She let out a long sigh. "I just hope they don't give up."

One of the outlaws started toward them.

"This one is Hoy, he's the worst of all," Julia said quietly.

Hoy stood in front of the two women and looked down at them with an evil smile.

"Well, now, lookie here," he said. "You're both so purty that I don't know which one of you I'm goin' to want first." He grabbed his crotch, suggestively.

"I might want the young 'n first, seein' as she's been here 'n I been workin' me up a real want for her," Murray said.

"But Silas says we can't do nothin' to her, on account of he's wantin' to sell her back to her pappy." Hoy stared at Leah. "So that leaves you," he said. "I don't know how long Silas is goin' to say we can't do nothin' to neither one of you, but I reckon he'll let us have you before long. 'N when he does, why, me 'n you is goin' to have just lots of fun."

"Hoy, you and Murray get back over here 'n leave them women alone, for now," King called.

With a small, but fiendish laugh, Hoy walked away from Leah and Julia.

"For now," Leah said.

"What?"

"He said leave us alone for now."

"I'm afraid," Julia said.

"I know," Leah said, as she turned her head away. She knew she couldn't let Julia see her cry.

Chapter Twenty

As Eagle Spring was between Jericho and the Devils River, Will decided they would stop there first. The first thing they needed to do was pay Buck for the gear he had provided them. And they wanted to tell Fred that King had broken out of jail yet again and he should be on the lookout for him. Conversation between the two brothers was limited as they held their horses at a trot for nearly the entire distance between the two points.

"Does something seem a little strange to you, Big Brother," Gid asked as they approached the way station. "No smoke, nobody movin' around, even the chickens aren't out scratching."

"I'd say, you're borrowing trouble, but the truth is, I'm feeling a little spooked myself," Will said as he put his hand on his pistol.

"Will, look!" Gid said sharply, as he raised his arm to

point to something lying on the ground.

"It's a body, it's ... damn, it's Buck!"

The two brothers broke into a gallop, then swung down from their saddles and rushed toward the man on the ground.

"Mr. Godfrey?" Will called out.

There were three bullet holes in his body, one in each knee and one in his chest. He was obviously very dead.

"What happened here? Where are Leah and Fred?" Will asked.

"Will, you don't ..." Gid paused in mid-sentence before he completed the sentence, "You don't think Fred did this, do you?"

"No, I ... Lord, Gid, I hope not."

"Well where are they?"

"I don't know. They may be holed up somewhere and if they are, I don't blame them. LEAH!" he shouted at the top of his voice. "FRED!"

"Help!"

"Will, did you hear that?"

"Help!"

"That's Fred," Will said. "Fred, where are you?"

"*Help,*" Fred called again, but his voice seemed muffled.

"We can hear you, Fred, tell us where you are?" Will repeated.

"In the well! I'm in the well!"

Again the voice was muffled and difficult to understand.

"Try again! Where are you?" Will called back.

"I'm in the well."

"Damn, little brother, it sounds like he said he was in the well."

Will and Gid hurried over to the well and looked down inside, but it was too dark to see all the way to the bottom.

"Fred? You down there?" Gid called down into the black maw.

"I'm here!" Fred called up. "Get me out of here!"

It took only a few minutes to send the bucket down the well and pull Fred up with the rope.

Fred sat down once they had him out and he leaned back against the stone top of the well.

"I've been down there for hours."

"Well, you're out now. Tell us what happened? Do you know Buck is dead and Leah doesn't seem to be around?" Will asked.

"It was Silas King. I thought he was in jail, but it was him and his men who did this. Poor Buck," he said as he looked over to the body lying there. "What happened?'

"King's men killed the deputy and then busted him out of jail," Gid said.

"They took Leah!"

"Are you sure?"

"They didn't know I was down in the well, so they

were just talking away. I heard 'em when they took her."

"Do you think you're up to riding? They probably took Leah to their hideout and I don't think they'll be expecting us. At least not so soon."

"Damn right I'm ready to ride," Fred said. "Those sons of bitches took Leah and if they've done anything to her, I'll kill every damn one of 'em."

Outlaw Hideout

"We need a new place," King said.

"What's wrong with this place?" Hoy asked.

"Too many people know about it," King said."

"How can that be? With the canyon and the river, why if anybody comes this way, we'd know about it and we'd take 'em out."

"Bell knows exactly where it is."

"Bell? Hell, we ain't got nothin' to worry about with him. We didn't see him at the way station and if he was there, he run like a scalded chicken. When we took the woman, he would'a come out if he weren't so scared. I say he's dead," Chiles said.

"He may be dead and maybe he's not. But the Crocketts sure knowed how to come after me. Now, how did they know about this place, if Bell didn't tell 'em?"

"You ain't gonna find a place as good as this," Chiles said.

"Hid away, only one-way in. Even if they did come, where else could be any better to kill 'em? We can stand guard."

"I think I know of a place," King said.

"When ya gonna find this place?" Baker asked.

"I'm goin' right now," King said. "Chiles, I want you and Hoy to come with me. The place I'm thinkin' about ain't nobody hardly even heard of, 'cause it ain't even on the map."

"What's the name of it?" Chiles asked.

"To tell the truth, I don't know what they're a' callin' it," King answered. "But it's full of people who don't wanna be found, just like us."

"Ya mean it's a outlaw camp."

"It may be more of a outlaw town," King said. "Kincaid, I want you and the girl you brung, to come with us."

"What about the other one?" Hoy asked. "Will we be takin' her too?"

"No, she'll stay here with the rest of the boys," King said.

"Please, please let me stay here with Leah," Julia pleaded.

"You ain't got no say, girl. She ain't worth nothin' but you are, so I don't care what the hell happens to her," King said. "But when we get to the new place, iffin the boys want to bring her up, they can."

"Take me too," Leah asked. "Julia is so young; I can

help look after her."

"I said you're stayin' here," King insisted. "Kincaid, get your girl."

"Don't do this," Julia said as Kincaid untied the ropes. "Please let us be together."

"Shut up," Kincaid said.

"No, I won't. Either leave me or take her."

Kincaid slapped Julia as hard as he could. "Now, shut up, or you'll get more of that."

"You didn't have to do that," Leah scolded.

King pointed to Leah. "Woman, you'd best hold your tongue. This girl's Papa's got a lot of money and when he gets to thinkin' there's no way, she's still alive, we'll send him a bill for takin' such good care of her. But you, your papa's dead, so who's willin' to pay for you?"

"Leah!" Julia called out in dread and uneasiness, as she stretched her arm toward her.

"It'll be all right, honey" Leah replied. "Have faith and pray, it'll be all right."

With tears of fear and concern streaming down her face, Julia stood by while Kincaid saddled her horse. Once she was mounted, he dropped a rope around her waist.

"You try 'n run off, 'n I'll jerk you right on your ass," Kincaid promised.

Baker, Liddell, Murray and Jones waited for about an

hour after King and the others left, then Baker brought up the subject they were all thinking about.

"You know what, there ain't no need to go to town to get us a whore, when we got us a woman right here," Baker said.

"I don't know," Jones said. "King didn't say nothin' 'bout us bein' able to use her."

"Yeah, that's just the point," Baker said. "He didn't say nothin', which means we can do whatever we want to do with her."

"I don't know," Liddell said. "She ain't no whore."

"So?"

"I mean, hell, like as not she don't have no idea in hell what to do."

Baker laughed at Liddell. "That's when it's the most fun when they're fresh, 'n ain't never done it before. You get to teach her."

"I don't want to teach her nothin'. I want her to know what she's doin'."

"I tell you what, I'll go first, 'n I'll teach her for you. Then after me, Murray 'n Jones can go so that by the time it's your time, she'll be broke in just real good. Why, she'll know most as much as any whore."

The four men were gathered in the far corner of the cabin and they were talking so quietly that Leah couldn't hear them. But they were laughing gruffly and looking at her with what could only be described as lascivious expressions.

"You boys go on outside. I don't need none of you watchin' while I break this girl in."

The three of them stepped out to the front of the cabin.

"You know she ain't goin' to let Baker do it without fightin' 'im," Liddell said.

"Oh hell, that's when it's the most fun," Jones said. "You take whores now. They do it all the time so they don't never feel nothin' 'n they don't hardly move none. Mostly they don't do nothin' but just lay there 'till you're done."

Will, Gid, and Fred were following Devils River. They were making no effort to keep their advance hidden because they were sacrificing stealth for speed. They knew that Leah was a captive of King and his gang and their primary mission was to rescue her.

They dismounted about a hundred yards before they actually reached the cabin, then continued forward, on foot. Fred, who was carrying a rifle, told them that they could probably get within twenty yards before they would have to come out into the open.

When they reached the cabin, they saw three men standing out front.

"You men, get your hands up!" Will called out.

"What the hell?" one of the men shouted.

Two of the men pulled their guns and began firing. Will and Gid returned fire and the two men went down. The third man rushed back into the cabin

"What is it?" Baker asked. "What's going on out there?"

Baker had not yet had time to give Leah her lesson, though he did have her tied to the bed, with her arms and legs spread.

"It's the Crockets," Liddell said. "And they've got Bell with 'em."

"Thank you, God, Fred is alive," Leah whispered as she closed her eyes. "This nightmare may soon be over."

"What about Murray and Jones?" Baker asked.

"They was shot 'n both of 'em went down. I reckon they're dead," Liddell said.

"Well we ain't," Baker said as he began cutting the ropes holding Leah.

Will and Gid still had their smoking pistols in their hands, studying the cabin where one of the three men had run.

"Don't you think we'd better get back behind those rocks, if the rest of them are in the cabin?" Fred asked. "I expect we're going to commence shooting here in a minute."

"Not yet," Gid said. "We can't go shooting up the cabin if Leah's in there."

"If they've hurt her . . ." Fred said, leaving the sentence

uncompleted.

At that moment the door opened and three people came out.

"Leah!" Fred said.

It was then that he saw there were two men with Leah and one of them, had his pistol pointed at Leah's head.

"I suppose you folks see what we've got here," Liddell said. "The Eagle Spring woman." Liddell was holding his gun to her head. "You let us ride away from here, 'n once we know we're safe, we'll let her go."

"Leah, is anyone else in the cabin?" Will called.

"No," Leah called back.

"Woman, keep your mouth shut," Baker said.

"I've got a good bead on Liddell," Fred said quietly. Fred was behind a rock, steadying his rifle on the rock. He was also in position to have a better angle on Liddell than either Will or Gid.

"All right," Will said. "Take your shot."

Fred pulled the trigger and the crack of the rifle echoed and re-echoed back from the flanking canyon wall. Liddell went down with blood spurting from the side of his head where it splattered Leah's dress.

"Ahh!" Leah said in shock.

"What the hell!" Baker shouted, throwing his gun down and raising his hands. "I give up!"

"Leah!" Fred shouted running toward her. Leah met

him with open arms and held him in a welcome and thankful embrace.

Will and Gid, keeping their gun on Baker, joined them.

"Leah, are you all right?" Will asked.

"I'm . . . not hurt," she said.

"Did they . . ." Fred started, but stopped, leaving the question hanging.

"They didn't rape me if that's what you were going to ask. But this one was about to when we heard the shooting outside."

"Thank God we got here in time," Fred said as he hugged her to him.

"Will, Gid, they have Julia."

"What?" Will replied with a gasp. The revelation hit him like a blow to the stomach. "Who has her?"

"King and Kincaid is part of his gang."

"I knew it, I never trusted that son of a bitch from the first time I saw him," Gid said.

"Is Julia all right. Has she been hurt? Have they . . ." Will asked.

"She hasn't been hurt and, so far at least, she hasn't been raped. I believe it's King's intention to sell her back to her father."

"Same as when he held up the stagecoach," Gid said.

"Yes. It was Kincaid who told King, Julia would be on the coach. I guess he didn't know about you two being with her," Leah said.

"I'm not surprised," Gid said.

"Leah, do you have any idea where they might have taken her?" Will asked.

"I don't know, I'm sorry. All he said was that it was a town that nobody had ever heard of."

"Fred, can you take care of Leah and . . . what's this one's name?"

"Val Baker," Fred said.

"Can you take care him?"

"You know I can. If he moves a muscle, I'll kill him."

"What about the rest of 'em?" Gid asked, taking in the three dead bodies with a wave of his hand?"

"We'll leave 'em be for now. If we come back this way and the critters haven't eaten them, we'll throw 'em in the ground. Right now, we don't have time to lose," Will said "Where are your horses?"

Baker remained silent.

"There's a lean-to behind the cabin," Leah said. She smiled. "You're going to be happy when you go out there."

"Will, I think we should check the saddlebags," Gid said as they approached the lean-to. "King had his share of the bank loot with him and I expect these men did as well."

"We'll look, but they may have buried it out here somewhere," Will said as he stepped around behind the shed.

A big smile crossed Will's face. "Look at those beautiful animals."

Gid pushed Will to the side. "Pepper, Scout, we've found you!"

The two horses, hearing familiar voices, began moving their head up and down.

"I wish I had an apple," Gid said as he began loosening the tethers that held the horses close.

"There's our tack," Will said, pointing to two saddles that were under the lean-to. "But the long guns are gone."

"Yes, but they didn't take anything else," Gid said as he went through his saddle bag.

"While we're here, let's go through these, too."

When they were finished, they had recovered a little over thirty-five hundred dollars.

"More for the good people of Commerce," Will said.

When the horses were bridled and saddled, Will led Scout, while Gid had Pepper.

"Leah, if we can find a lead line, can you manage taking your two horses back with you?" Will asked.

"I won't need a lead line, they'll follow me," Leah said confidently. "And it's more than likely the other three horses will follow as well."

"All right. You two go on back to Jericho, and Fred, I want you to take Baker and this money to Sheriff O'Shea," Will said.

"Uh, do you think that's a good idea?" Leah asked. "I mean, for Fred to go to the sheriff."

"We have no choice," Will said. "We can't just let Baker go, and I don't think any of us want to shoot him in cold blood do we?"

Chapter Twenty-one

Long Trail Ranch

John and Ethyl Abernathy along with their foreman were sitting in the living room listening to the rich tones of the music box which not only provided music but looked like a beautiful piece of furniture. The deep, resonate tones of the box seemed to reflect the sadness that the Abernathys had felt since their daughter's disappearance.

"Leo," John said when the music finished, "did you have any idea that Kincaid was capable of doing such a thing?"

"Yes, sir, I have to say that I thought he was capable of doing what he did."

"I just hope and pray that no harm has come to our baby," Ethyl said, as she took her ever present handkerchief and wiped her eyes. "And, if she has married Kincaid, I hope she knows that we still love her. I'd hate for her to think she could never come home again."

"She's a young girl and that polecat Kincaid took advantage of her. But I've known Julia since she was a toddler and I know how much she loves both of you and this ranch, too. You'll be seeing her again, I just know you will and she'll tell you how much she loves you."

"Thank you for those words," Ethyl said. "I . . . we both needed a little lift in our spirits and we knew we could get that from you." Ethyl smiled. "And I had Maria make a pie just for you."

"That's great and I'll even share it with the two of you," Leo said with a little laugh. John and Ethyl laughed as well.

"Thank you, Leo. I believe that may be the first time I've laughed since this whole ordeal began," Ethyl said.

With Julia

McKittrick Creek was flowing briskly, rising above ground at several points between rock layers, then returning below ground for several hundred feet before emerging again. King, Chiles, Hoy, Kincaid and Julia were following the creek north through McKittrick Canyon. Julia was glad for the creek because it provided a steady source of fresh water. Also, she thought if she ever had a chance to escape, she could follow this creek back to where she might run into someone who knew Long Trail Ranch.

Long Trail Ranch. How she missed it now. She wondered what her Mama and Papa were doing right now. Leah had told her that the Crockett brothers were looking for her and she was sure that her father was paying them. Of course, he would. She knew that her parents loved her, no matter that she had defied them to do such a foolish thing as run away with Kincaid. How could she have been such a fool?

"Mama, Papa, if I get out of this, I want you to know that I love you and I'll never do anything like this again." Julia said the words aloud, though so quietly no one could have heard her.

"Let's stop here and eat," King said.

"Ha, ain't got much to fix," Baker said. "Bacon, some taters, 'n some flour that's got weevils in it."

"We'll use that for supper," King said. "All we're goin' to eat now is some jerky."

"Well, hell, boss, we don't even need to stop for that," Chiles said. "We could eat that without ever leavin' our saddle."

"Eatin' ain't the only reason we're stoppin'," King said. "We need to give the horses a break, 'n beside that, I got to take a piss, 'n I expect I ain't the only one."

"You got that right," Kincaid said.

"Hoy," King said as they mounted. "we ain't to far from Salcedo and I'm thinkin' it's about time to get shed of this here girl. They got a telegraph operator in Salcedo, so's it's time to get in touch with Abernathy. You go over there and tell 'im if he wants to see her alive again, it's goin' to cost him ten thousand dollars."

"Hell, Silas, you can't send a telegram like that," Chiles said.

"Why not?" Hoy asked. "If it was only me, I'd be askin' for twenty thousand."

"Abernathy won't be the only one a' readin' it. The telegrapher in Salcedo will read it, 'n so will the one in Toyah. One of 'em is goin' to go to the sheriff," Chiles said.

"How else do you think we can get word to 'im then?" King asked.

"You can do it by telegram, but you got to word it so's only Abernathy will know what you're a sayin'."

"All right, Chiles, you go send the telegram," King said. "But somehow you need to tell him that we've got the girl, 'n it's goin' to cost him ten thousand dollars to get her back."

"I'll do it," Chiles said.

Eagle Spring Way Station

"What do you want to do about your pa?" Fred asked

237

when he, Leah, and Baker returned to the way station.

"I want to hook up the buckboard and take him into town to the undertaker. I want him to have a proper burial."

"All right, we'll do that."

An hour later they started toward Jericho, with Leah driving the buckboard. Fred was riding in back with Buck Godfrey's body and a bound up Val Baker.

"Leah, we'll be coming into town, soon," Fred said, about two and a half hours after they left. "Where do you want to go?"

"I want to go to the sheriff's office first," Leah called back. "I want enough time to be able to make arrangements for Papa's funeral without having to worry about a prisoner."

At first, the buckboard just looked like any of the other wagons, buckboards and surreys that made up the traffic on the busy street. But one sharp-eyed individual noticed that one of the two men sitting in back, was tied up. Then, another noticed a body lying in back of the buckboard, and the curiosity grew. By the time the buckboard stopped in front of the sheriff's office, the number of the curious had grown from three or four to ten, or more.

Sheriff O'Shea, his attention arrested by what was going on outside his very door, stepped outside.

"Miss Godfrey," he said. "What do you have here?"

"This is one of the men who murdered my father and took me prisoner," Leah said.

"Your father was murdered? Oh, dear, I'm sorry to hear that," Sheriff O'Shea said.

"He's also one of the men who robbed the bank in Commerce," Fred added.

"Well, bring him in," Sheriff O'Shea said, stepping back inside, holding the door open.

"Fred, I'm going to take Papa down to the mortuary," Leah said.

"All right, I'll be right here when you come back," Fred said.

"Sheriff, I think there's somethin' you should know about this man," Baker said when he was taken inside. "Me 'n him was together in the King gang, 'n he helped us rob the train."

The sheriff turned to Fred with a quizzical look on his face.

"Here's some of the money that was taken from the bank in Commerce," Fred said. "Three thousand, five hundred and sixty-seven dollars."

"Where's the rest of it? There was close to ten thousand dollars took in that holdup."

"He kept the rest of it, Sheriff," Baker said pointing at Fred. "It's like I told you, he was part of the gang. He's givin' you this money to make you think he's honest, only he ain't."

"He's lyin' to you, Sheriff," Fred said. "I don't have the rest of the money. Will and Gid Crockett, 'n I killed the ones that were with Baker. There were three more of them and we went through their saddlebags." Fred pointed to the money that was now lying on the sheriff's desk. "This is all the money we found. King and the others rode off with the rest of the money, and with Julia Abernathy."

"Julia? Do you mean Colonel Abernathy's girl that's been missin'?"

"Yes."

"He was in on that too, Sheriff," Baker said. "I'm tellin' you, he's part of the gang. He just turned on the rest of us so he could have all the rest of the money from the bank."

"Is he telling the truth? Did you take part in the train holdup?" Sheriff O'Shea asked.

"There was no holdup," Fred said.

"I'll tell you something else," Baker said. "They's paper out on him in Kansas. He's a wanted man."

"Is there paper out on you in Kansas?"

"There may be," Fred admitted.

"What do you mean, there may be?"

"I ... I rode with Quantrill. I understand there's paper out on everyone who rode for Quantrill."

"They's a five hunnert dollar reward out for him," Baker said. "All you have to do is get him moved to Kansas and the five hunnert dollar reward is yours."

"I'm an officer of the law, I can't collect a reward for criminals I arrest."

"You ain't a lawman in Kansas," Baker offered.

Sheriff O'Shea stroked his chin. "No, I'm not. I tell you what, I think I'm going to lock you both up until I do a little more checkin' on all this."

As Bell was pleading his case with Sheriff O'Shea, Leah was at the undertaker's building, making arrangements for the funeral and burial of her father. At the moment, Buck Godfrey, whose given name was Boston Neil Godfrey, was lying on a metal table. George Ford was showing Leah the coffins he had available.

"For a man of your father's status, only the best would be good enough for him, and that would be this one." Ford rubbed his hand on the outside of a shiny black coffin. "This beauty was shipped all the way from St. Louis, and it's called the 'Eternal Cloud'. Wouldn't this be the perfect casket for Mr. Godfrey when he enters his eternity?"

"No, I think my father would like this one," Leah said as she ran her hand over a wood casket. She wished that she could ask Fred to make a casket for her father, but there was no time for him to do it.

"All right, will you be making the arrangements for the funeral and the burial?"

"Yes, I would like it to be tomorrow morning, if possible."

"I think he'll be ready," Ford said. "I'll get a grave opened this afternoon."

When Leah returned to the sheriff's office, she was shocked to learn that Fred was in jail.

"What? What for? Why have you put him in jail?"

"Baker says that Bell was a member of King's gang and that he brought him in just to keep his ownself from going to jail."

"Sheriff, did Fred not turn over money from the bank robbery in Commerce? Doesn't that prove he isn't one of them?"

"There was close to ten thousand dollars took from the Commerce bank; Bell didn't even bring in half of it. Where's the rest of the money?"

"That's because King and the others took their half of the money and went their own way, leaving, Baker and three more behind."

"Wait a minute, how is it that you know so much about this?" Sheriff O'Shea asked.

"I know about the gang because I was there," Leah said. "When they killed my father, they took me for God only knows what purpose. It was Fred who rescued me from them."

"You said there was three others? Where'd they go?"

"They're all dead. Fred and the Crocketts killed them."

Sheriff O'Shea shook his head. "You're being awful protective of this here Bell. What's that about?"

"Because he is an innocent man," Leah said.

"So, you say," the sheriff said. "Now, tell me how come I didn't know you was captured? How come your pa didn't send no telegram?"

Leah let out an exasperated sigh. "Because he was dead. They left him lying on the ground when they took me. And then when we got to their cabin, they forced me to sit on the floor tied to Julia Abernathy."

"Well now, that's where I've got you, missy" Sheriff O'Shea said with a triumphant grin. "Are you sure you ain't makin' this whole thing up? I know for a fact that that girl run off of her own accord with one of her pa's hired hands."

"Yes, she did. It was Jamie Kincaid, but he betrayed her. When King and his bunch rode off, Kincaid was with him and he took Julia with him."

"There ya go. Maybe the girl wanted to go with her man," the sheriff said.

"With a rope tied around her? I don't think so," Leah said. "I'll be back for Mr. Bell, when you have this all figured out as you say, but right now I have to plan a funeral."

Chapter Twenty-two

Although they still didn't know where Julia was, Will believed they had made a rather significant step in their search. They now knew she was alive and that she was with King. Because King's nose was such a distinctive feature, he was not likely to be forgotten if anyone saw him and would leave more of a trail, if not an actual trail, a trail of contacts.

Will and Gid began following the river in search of the gang. Even if they had been trying to track them physically, it would have been very difficult because the path alongside the river was almost pure rock. And because the rock wasn't one smooth pathway, they had to ride carefully.

Just before nightfall, they saw a campfire ahead. Dismounting, and tethering their horses, they crept ahead on foot.

There was one man sitting at the campfire.

"You boys can come on in, if you want to," the man called out, calmly, surprising Will that he had seen them.

Will and Gid exchanged a glance, then walked on up to the campfire. The man sitting at the fire looked to be in his sixties, perhaps even his seventies. He had long white hair and a white beard. His wrinkled face had been darkened by the sun.

"Where's your horses?" the man asked.

"We tethered them back a ways."

"Thought you might have. Do either of you have any coffee?"

"Yes, we have coffee."

"I kilt me a rabbit a while ago 'n I'm fixin' to put 'im on to cook. You share some of your coffee, 'n I'll share my rabbit."

Will and Gid smiled.

"I'll bring up the horses," Will said.

"They call me Beans," the old man said after the horses were brought up, the rabbit cooking and the coffee started.

"I appreciate you sharing your fire and your rabbit with us, Beans," Will said.

"I been out of coffee for some time now," Beans said. "I figure we're comin' out about even. You boys will be ridin' on? Or are you planning on spendin' the night, 'cause iffin you are, why you're welcome to share m' fire."

"We appreciate your hospitality, Beans, and I think we'll take you up on your offer," Will said.

"It's good to have you. Not just because you brung coffee, but because it's good to have someone to talk to, other 'n Rhoda. She's a good listener, but she don't talk much." He pointed to his mule.

Gid laughed. "Now Beans, what would you do if she *did* talk to you?"

"I'd figure I was drunk, even though I ain't had me enough whiskey to get drunk in a coon's age."

"What are you doing out here, all alone?" Will asked.

"Well, ever' body's got to be somewhere, 'n this is my somewhere," Beans answered. "so why are you two out here in the middle of nowhere?"

"We're looking for some men who robbed a bank here awhile back," Will said. "And now they have a girl with them."

"You say there's a outlaw girl with the gang?" Beans asked, surprised by the revelation."

"No, no, she's not one of 'em. She's a little sixteen-year-old girl that they're holding a prisoner."

"Those evil bastards," Beans said. "I hope you find them."

"We will," Gid said, resolutely.

"Which brings us to the question. Have you seen anyone pass through here in the last two days?" Will asked.

Beans shook his head. "I'm sorry, I ain't seen no one," he said. "But," he was quick to add, "that don't mean they ain't come, 'cause I ain't always right in this particular spot so's I could keep a eye on the trail. Sometimes I've gone back into thicket so's to get a rabbit, or a squirrel, or maybe a bird of some kind. So they could 'a got through when I warn't here."

"If they did go through here, do you have any idea where they might have gone?"

A broad smile spread across Bean's face. "Maybe Salcedo. It's 'bout fifteen maybe twenty miles on down the river."

"So there *is* a town south of here." It was an affirmation, not a question and Gid's mood was lifted by the information.

"Yeah, they don't hardly nobody know about it. I went there three maybe four years ago when I had to pick up a little money. I sharpen knives, I do."

"Why don't you come along with us tomorrow?" Will invited. "We'll buy you some coffee, and maybe a few bullets."

"You don't have to do nothin' like that," Beans replied, in a voice that suggested he was just saying that because he thought it would be polite.

Chapter Twenty-three

While Will and Gid were following the Devils River south into Salcedo, King, Chiles, Hoy and Kincaid, along with their prisoner, followed the McKittrick Canyon for three days and two nights, reaching the town of Diablo, early in the evening of the third day.

If someone looked on the map for Diablo, Texas, they wouldn't find it. If someone asked the authorities in Austin about the town of Diablo, no one would have an answer. There was no record of any such town and yet when King's men rode into Diablo, it most certainly did exist.

The town was alive with commerce: it had a grocery store, a blacksmith shop, a livery, a gunsmith and at least four saloons. King led the little group to the front of a building called the Two Bit Saloon.

As the men dismounted, Kincaid took the rope off Julia. "Don't give us no trouble in here," he said.

"I can't go in here," Julia said. "Papa would never allow it."

Kincaid laughed. "Your ole' man ain't here, 'n what he don't know, won't hurt him. Now, get in there," he ordered.

Kincaid grabbed Julia's arm and forced her through the swinging batwing doors of the saloon.

As soon as they stepped into the saloon, they were greeted by a woman who didn't look like any woman Julia had ever seen. Her blouse was cut so scandalously low that her breasts were visible all the way to the nipples. Her face was painted, she was wearing bright red lip rouge and her eyes were lined in black.

"Well, what have we here? Have you men brought your own woman?" she asked, eyeing Julia curiously.

"No, darlin', you're the one I want," Hoy said, taking the bar girl by the arm and starting toward the back of the saloon.

Other bar girls came. One took Chiles, and the other looked at Kincaid, who at the moment was holding onto Julia's arm. The soiled dove looked at Julia.

"Honey, do you mind if I take your boyfriend for a little poke? Or are you the jealous type?"

"He's not my boyfriend."

"Come on, I'll go with you," Kincaid said. He pointed to Julia. "Don't you go nowhere."

"Where could I go?" Julia asked.

Julia didn't know if this ordeal would ever end. They said they were going to contact her father to ask for ransom. How much would they demand? Would he be able to pay what they would ask? If not, what would happen?

"Come upstairs with me, honey," one of the bar girls said to Julia.

"What?" Julia asked, surprised by the woman's invitation.

The woman nodded toward King. "The big man there, the one with two noses, wants a poke, so he's going with Millie and he's paying me the same as I would get for an all nighter, just to keep an eye on you tonight. My name's Cindy. What's yours?"

"My name's Julia. I . . . I don't want to go with you."

"Honey, it's either come with me, or you'll have to go up with one of these men. It's your choice."

Julia nodded her head.

Cindy led Julia up the stairs then into a room. She closed the door behind her.

"I'll tell you the truth. I didn't know what the big guy had in mind when he hired me, but I'm glad to watch after you instead of working tonight," Cindy said.

"What kind of work do you do?" Julia asked.

Cindy got a surprised look on her face. "Honey, you've been with these men all this time and you don't know what I do? Didn't your mother ever tell you what men and women do together?"

Julia thought of her experience in the loft with Kincaid. That was her only experience with a man.

"I'm a . . . well, men pay me to come up here and we . . . uh . . ." Cindy stammered.

"Oh! You mean men pay you to do *that*?"

Cindy chuckled, then put her hand on Julia's cheek. "Bless you, child, you really are the innocent one aren't you?"

Julia didn't answer.

"What I want to know is, what are you doing with all those men? They don't look like a men's church group."

"I was captured," Julia said.

"Captured?"

"Well, not really. It was my own fault. I thought I was in love with Jamie and I ran away from Mama and Papa to be with him. But he . . .." Julia began crying, unable to finish the sentence.

"You mean you are their prisoner?" Cindy asked, shocked at the revelation.

Unable to verbalize an answer, Julia simply nodded. Then, finally she was able to speak.

"They're going to ask my father to pay a ransom before they'll let me go home."

"Will your father be able to do that?"

"Papa is a very wealthy man. But I don't think he knows where I am. Oh, Cindy, can you tell the sheriff about me? He could send a wire to Papa and . . ."

Cindy was shaking her head no, before Julia was even able to finish her sentence.

"Sweetheart, we don't have a sheriff. We don't have any law at all in this town."

"Well, can you send Papa a telegram, tell him where I am so he can tell Will and Gid where to come after me?"

Again, Cindy shook her head. "We don't have a telegraph. We aren't even a real town. Almost everyone you see in town is an outlaw, except for the ones who make money off the outlaws. And you might even say they're outlaws, too. I'm sorry there's nothing I can do for you."

Julia dropped her head in despair. She knew the time was running short and so far, except for Leah telling her that the Crocketts were looking for her, she had not had one word of encouragement. Cindy had just confirmed that she was in a den of thieves, that not even the state of Texas knew of the whereabouts of this place.

Cindy smiled. "No, that's not true, I can do some things for you." She pointed to the bed. "How long has it been since you slept in a bed?"

"A long time," Julia said looking longingly at the bed.

"And when is the last time you had a meal other than beans and bacon?"

"Oh, it's been forever."

Cindy held up her hand. "If you promise me you won't try and run away while I'm gone, I'll go downstairs and get you a real supper. I know Frederica fried chicken tonight. There may even be some potatoes, too."

"That sounds heavenly," Julia said, "but I don't have any money to pay you."

"Don't you worry about that. The two nosed man paid me enough that I can get supper for both of us. You wait right here; I'll be back before you know it."

Julia sat on the bed after Cindy left. She was alone. This was the first time since she had run away from home that she had been totally alone and she welcomed the solitude.

Cindy came back less than five minutes later carrying two plates filled with food.

"Oh, Cindy, excuse me, but I'm afraid I'm going to eat like a pig, it's been so long." Julia said as she grabbed for a drumstick.

"Gobble away, honey," Cindy said with a smile.

The two ate their meals, Julia as she had warned, ate ravenously.

"When is the last time you had a bath and changed your clothes?" Cindy asked.

"I don't know," Julia said. "It's been a lot of days, maybe even two or three weeks or more. I've lost track of time."

Cindy smiled. "How would you like to take a bath?"

"Oh, Cindy, yes!" Julia said enthusiastically. "Short of going home, I can't think of anything I'd rather do, than take a bath." She looked down at herself. "Even if I have to put on my same dirty clothes."

"Maybe I can take care of that as well," Cindy said. "We're about the same size, I'm sure I can find something for you to wear."

"Thanks, Cindy, but . . . uh," Julia replied without completing her sentence.

For a moment, Cindy was confused by Julia's hesitancy, then realizing what Julia was thinking, Cindy laughed out loud.

"Oh, I know what you're thinking." She passed her hand down over her very provocative clothing. "These are my working clothes. I never leave here wearing something like this. I've got some clothes so normal you could wear 'em to church, and I would, if we had a church here," she finished with a smile. "Let me get you set up with a bath, then we'll work on your clothes."

Half an hour later, a tub, hot water and soap had been brought up to Cindy's room. After the men who delivered the tub left, Cindy went over to lock the door.

"This will prevent us from having any unannounced visitors."

When Julia slipped her whole body down into the hot water, the only word she could think of was blissful. She just sat there until the water began to lose some of its heat and only then did she apply soap and wash her hair and her body. When she stepped out of the tub, she felt completely re-invigorated.

Cindy met her with a spread open towel.

"Thanks," Julia said.

"I've laid out some clothes for you on the bed," Cindy said, indicating them by spreading out her arm.

Julia glanced toward them with some apprehension then, when she saw that they were indeed regular street clothes she smiled.

"Oh, thank you," Julia said. "Thank you for the supper, for the bath, for the clothes and thank you for being so nice."

Julia put on the clothes Cindy had provided, then looked at herself in the mirror.

"You're right, Cindy, you could go to church in these clothes. I could sit in our pew with Mama and . . ." Julia choked up for a moment, then barely squeezed out the word, "Papa."

Tears that she didn't know she still had left began to stream down her cheeks.

"Oh, Julia, I am so sorry," Cindy said, and she took Julia in a warm embrace.

Julia, wearing the clothes Cindy had given her, lay down on the bed and soon, because of her exhausted condition, and because it was the first bed she had been on in weeks, she was soon fast asleep.

Cindy looked at the young woman lying on her bed and thought of her own, sweet sister. Cindy, whose real name was Mary Beth Collins, had left home after being raped by her uncle. Neither her mother nor father had believed her and they had forced her to leave home. After nearly starving to death in low paying jobs, she, too, was abducted and forced to work in a house of prostitution. But she believed her sister was still at home and by now, would be about Julia's age.

What if her sister was in the same situation as Julia?

Cindy decided she was in a position to do whatever she could to help Julia escape. Leaving her asleep in the bed, she started to plan her mission.

Chapter Twenty-four

Earlier, that same day

When Chiles rode into Salcedo, his first thought wasn't to send a telegram. His first thought was to get a beer to wash down the trail dust, then have himself a really good dinner. And why not? He had a saddle bag full of money, and an appetite born of two weeks of nothing but beans, bacon, and jerky.

The first restaurant he rode by was a Mexican restaurant and he was drawn to it by the savory aromas that drifted out onto the street. He stopped out front, secured his horse to the hitching rail, then stepped inside.

"*Bienvenido señor*," a young woman, said, by way of greeting. "*Deseas cenar con nosotros?*"

"I don't speak no Mex," Chiles said.

"I'm sorry, Senor," the woman said in heavily accented

English. "Do you want to eat?"

"Why else would I come in here?" Chiles asked with a snarl.

Chiles ordered enchiladas and refried beans. Then, as he awaited his meal, he composed the telegraph.

FOUND LOST DAUGHTER WILL REUNITE WITH FAMILY COLLECT $20000 REWARD RESPOND KC IN SALCEDO

Jericho

With Fred in jail, and burial arrangements completed for her father, Leah took the buckboard out to Long Trail Ranch. When she stopped just in front of the porch steps, she was met by one of the ranch cowboys.

"Can I help you, ma'am?"

"I'd like to see Mr. Abernathy, please."

"Yes, ma'am, he's home. Just go on up there 'n knock. I'll take care of your team and buckboard for you."

"Thank you," Leah said.

A Mexican woman answered the knock, then invited her in to stand in the front hall while she summoned John. A moment later a tall man with a van dyke beard came to meet her with a questioning expression on his face.

"Yes, ma'am," he said. "Is there something I can do for you?"

258

"Colonel Abernathy, my name is Leah Godfrey. My father and I run—that is, we ran the Eagle Springs Way Stop on the Texas and Pacific Railroad."

"Yes, I know that stop."

Leah took a deep breath, then let it out in a long sigh. "Mr. Abernathy, until just a few days ago, I was being held captive by Silas King."

"The outlaw?"

"Yes, I was one of two captives he held. Your daughter was the other one."

"What?" The word exploded from John's mouth. "Ethyl!" he called. "Ethyl, get in here!"

An attractive, middle aged woman came hurrying to answer her husband's call. "John, what is it?" she asked.

John pointed at Leah.

"This woman says she was with Julia and that she's alive. Our baby is being held captive by Silas King."

"The outlaw?" Ethel questioned as she covered her mouth with her hand. "Is she all right?"

"When we were separated, she was fine, frightened and disillusioned of course, but basically she was all right."

"You say she is with Silas King. How did that happen?" John asked. "When she left here, her note said she was going with a man named Kincaid and I'm ashamed to say, it was of her own free will."

"Julia told me about that, but Kincaid betrayed her

trust. He was one of the members of King's gang all along and he brought your daughter to them. It is my understanding that they are holding her for ransom."

"This ransom, how much and where do I pay it?"

Leah shook her head. "I don't know the answer to your question."

"You say she is all right. Does that mean they haven't . . . uh . . ." Ethyl asked in a small voice.

"She had not been violated when we were separated."

"If you were both King's prisoners, how did you escape, but Julia didn't?"

Leah explained how King believed the cabin where the gang was hiding had been discovered and that he and half his gang, along with Kincaid and Julia, had gone to look for another place to hide out.

"Will and Gid Crockett and Fred Bell rescued me."

"Will and Gid Crockett? I hired them to find my daughter. Where are they now?" John asked.

"They arrived after Julia was already gone, but I believe they are very close to finding her."

"Oh, Lord, I pray that you are right," Ethyl said.

John put his arm around his wife. "Take some solace my dear, in knowing that they are close. I have faith that Will and Gid will find her."

"Young lady, Leah is it? Won't you please stay with us for awhile? I have a thousand questions to ask."

"I'd be honored, Mrs. Abernathy, but I must get back to Jericho," Leah said.

"A woman alone can't be driving a buckboard back to town at this time of day. Please stay for a bite to eat," Ethyl said. "And spend the night with us."

During their dinner Leo Hunter came into the dining room without knocking.

"John, I believe this is something you've been waiting for. When Danny brought the children home from school, he said this was for you." Leo handed over a yellow envelope that said Western Union on it.

John took it with trembling hands. "Leo, do you know what it says?"

"No, I didn't read it, but we can only hope it's from Julia."

John tore open the envelope and read:

IN SALCEDO CLOSE CROCKETTS

"Oh, John," Ethyl cried out. "What good news. I pray this will soon be over!"

After dinner, they gathered in the drawing room, the conversation was much more, cheery than it had been before the telegram.

"My dear, how terrible of us to keep pestering you with questions about Julia, when I'm sure you have told us all there is to tell," John said. "We would like to invite you to spend the night with us, that is, if you don't think your father would mind."

Leah's eyes clouded with tears. "My father was killed at the same time I was captured."

"Oh, you poor thing," Ethyl said. "Here we have been bombarding you with questions about our daughter, when you are dealing with your own grief."

"Nothing can be done for Papa now," Leah said, this time allowing the tears to fall, "but we still may be able to do something for Julia."

"I have faith in Will and Gid," John said. "I knew them during the war, before they . . . and I know what they are capable of doing."

"The death of your father is so recent. Were you able to have a proper burial for him?"

"Not yet. He is at the undertaker's place now. He is to be buried tomorrow."

"We would very much like to attend his funeral," John said, "that is if you don't mind."

"I would be honored to have you in attendance," Julia said.

Even though there was a guest bedroom, an unknown in most houses, Ethyl asked Leah to stay in Julia's room that night. "It would bring me some comfort to know you are using her bedroom and since you became friends with

Julia, it becomes even more meaningful."

Leah was pleased to be staying at the Abernathy's home, as she had been dreading going back to the way station without her father or Fred being there with her. She assumed the railroad would have put someone in place to handle the telegraph line and to make sure the tanks were full of water for the train. She only hoped that that person had found her beloved horses out back and was taking care of them.

When Leah entered Julia's bedroom, she was struck by the contrast to her own humble dwelling. Leah had a single bed, a chair and one small chest in her room.

By the light of an oil lamp that was made of cut crystal, Leah saw a canopied bed that had a pink bedspread, with ruffles. The mahogany dresser had a silver-lined mirror and on the dresser was a toilet set with a tortoise shell comb and a silver brush. Leah reached for the brush, but then she withdrew her hand.

"No, this is Julia's room," Leah said. "It should be exactly the way it was when she left it."

When she began to undress, she took off her shoes and it was then that she saw five pair of button shoes lined up next to a curved-door chifforobe. Leah examined her own shoes. The soles were nearly worn through but she would never have thought of having more than one pair of shoes at a time.

In that instant, her heart went out to Julia, to be used to a life like this and now be subjected to the ignominy of being a prisoner of a group of horrible men. What would have made Julia even consider running off with Jamie Kincaid? Her parents obviously loved her very much and there was nothing they wouldn't do for their daughter. Leah had no doubt that whatever the ransom Silas King demanded; it would be paid.

She had held back telling John and Ethyl the fact that Julia was being kept tied up to a stove leg and made to sit on the floor all the time. There were just some things they didn't need to know.

As Leah lay her head on the pillow, she said a quick prayer for Julia and for Fred. She must find a way to convince the sheriff he was a good person.

"The Crocketts will take care of it," she said, and then she fell asleep instantly.

Diablo

Julia was enjoying her first sleep in a bed since she had no idea how long, but she was awakened by a gentle shake of her shoulder.

"Wake up, honey, I'm going to help you get out of here."

"What?" Julia asked, still groggy with sleep.

"You want to get out of here? Come on, I'll help you,"

Cindy said.

"You would do that?" Julia asked, sitting up immediately.

"Wait here while I see if anyone is moving around," Cindy said, as she quietly moved to the door and looked out into the hallway.

"Come on," she whispered.

Cindy led Julia down the dark stairs and through the now deserted saloon to the swinging doors that led outside.

"Come," Cindy said, starting down the street.

"What about my horse?"

"Leave it. If they see your horse out here, they'll think you're still here. At least long enough to give us a head start."

"Us?"

"Yes, I'm coming with you," Cindy said. "Once they discover you're gone and I was the one who was supposed to be looking out for you, my life won't be worth anything."

"Are we walking?"

"No, I have a surrey," Cindy said.

On Devils River

Will, Gid and Beans awakened the next morning just as a resplendent band of color spread across the east, presaging the rising of the sun. Will and Gid walked down to the river to fill their canteens and listen to the song of the water as it broke white over the rocks.

"You reckon there's any trout in there?" Gid asked.

"If we had time, we could do a little fishing and find out," Will said.

Gid dipped his canteen into the fast-flowing water. "Big Brother, there is absolutely no way I would fish with you."

"What? Now why would you say that?"

"Because," Gid said, as he corked his canteen. "I don't know what it is about you, but as soon as you drop your hook in the water, all the fish run the other way."

"I smell the coffee," Will said.

Breakfast was jerky biscuits and coffee, supplied by Will and Gid and happily cooked by Beans.

The sun was four discs up from the horizon when the three men broke camp to begin their ride to Salcedo. It would take about six hours but would have been considerably faster had Will and Gid been alone. It was Bean's old mule that was slowing them considerably.

Long Trail Ranch

Leah awakened the next morning to the aroma of coffee and bacon. Her first night in a bed in over a week had given her a refreshing sleep. By the time she got downstairs, John and Ethyl were already sitting at the dining room table, drinking coffee.

"Good morning, dear," Ethyl said.

"Oh, have I missed breakfast?" Leah asked.

"No, we're just having an early cup of coffee," John said. "I want us to get to Jericho as early as possible. Didn't you say your father's service is scheduled for this morning?"

"Yes, it is," Leah said as she sat down at the table.

While they were eating, there was a knock on the door.

"That's strange," John said. "Who would be here at the crack of dawn?"

"Hurry, John, maybe it's news from Will and Gid," Ethyl said.

When John opened the door, Lenny Gilstrap, the telegraph operator, was standing there.

Lenny was smiling. "I figured I bring this out myself. I know how you've been a waiting a long time for this message."

John grabbed the telegram Lenny was holding and tore it open.

Ethyl and Leah watched anxiously as John removed the message. The expression on his face told them that it wasn't the message they were looking for.

John shared it with the others.

FOUND LOST DAUGHTER WILL REUNITE WITH FAMILY COLLECT $20000 REWARD RESPOND KC SALCEDO

"I don't understand," Ethyl said. "Have we offered a reward?"

"Kit Chiles," Leah said.

"What?"

"That message is from the kidnappers. I learned all their names while I was there. KC must be Kit Chiles. This is their ransom demand."

"I'll pay it," John said, resolutely. "If it will get my daughter back, I'll pay it."

"Colonel, I understand that you are willing to pay the ransom, but I'm suspicious that this came from Chiles and not King. I think you should ask him to verify that he has Julia."

"Yes, that's a good idea, young lady," John said. "Lenny, when we get to town I'll devise a message that only Julia will know the answer to. If you wait a minute, we'll ride back with you."

268

Chapter Twenty-five

Julia and Cindy had taken turns driving the surrey, one driving and the other sleeping.

They were heading south along McKittrick Creek and as the sun rose it turned from being a great orange ball, to a bright orb.

"I took some bread from the kitchen," Cindy said. "That will have to do for our breakfast and probably lunch, too. I wish I had gotten some coffee."

"Thanks to you and that wonderful supper last night, I'm not all that hungry," Julia said. "A little bread will be fine and coffee would be nice, but we've got the stream for water."

"That's true."

"Cindy, you took a great risk and I can't tell you how much I appreciate it."

"I'm a whore, honey, but I'm not without conscience."

"Where are we going? Do you have any place in mind?"

"To tell the truth, I don't have any idea where we're going. I only know where we didn't want to be. But if we follow the creek far enough, we are bound to come across someone who is not an outlaw. And I have a hundred and fifty dollars with me, so I'm hoping we can buy some food from somebody and maybe even some coffee, just enough to keep us going until we get to a town where we might find some law."

"Even better would be to find a telegraph office," Julia said. "I could send a wire to Papa and he could tell Will and Gid where to find us. Those are the men who are out looking for me."

"If these two really are looking for you, it would be good if it was them we ran into," Cindy said.

"Cindy, where will you go after we escape?"

"I don't know, I just know that I won't be able to go back home. But anyplace is better than where I was."

"What do you mean, she's gone?" King asked, angrily. "Her horse is still tied up out front."

"That's so," Kincaid said. "But the brat is gone."

"Find the whore. I paid that whore to keep an eye on her."

"The whore's gone too," Kincaid said.

"Damn it all to hell! Casey, what's going on here?" King

asked the saloon owner.

"Didn't you say the girl's ole' man was rich?" Casey asked.

"Yes."

"Then my guess is that Cindy's goin' to take her back for some kind of reward."

"Well, how hard will it be to find 'em?" King asked. "They'll both be on foot."

"Not likely," Casey said. "Cindy's got a surrey and a fine, high-steppin' horse."

"Do you have any idea where they might be goin'?"

"They had to go south along the creek," Casey said. If you go north, in about two or three miles from here, the canyon closes in on the creek and you can't get through, least wise not in a surrey."

"Come on, Kincaid, we're goin' south," King said.

"The sun is pretty hot," Julia said. "Would you mind stopping so I can get a drink of water?"

"Oh, bless me, what am I thinking of?" Cindy said. "I brought a canteen; we can fill it at the creek."

Cindy pulled the surrey to a stop, set the break and climbed down to go with Julia down to the water's edge. Even before they filled the canteen, they cupped their hands and scooped water up to drink. After a moment, Cindy reached down and, scooping up some water, threw it into Julia's face.

"Hey!" Julia said.

Cindy laughed and scooped up another handful of water and this time Julia sent some water toward Cindy. For fully thirty seconds they splashed water on each other, laughing as they did so.

Then, as they started back toward the surrey with the filled canteen, Julia looked over at the woman who had risked everything to save her. She could see where the water she had sent toward Cindy had dampened her clothes, and she felt her own wet clothes, then laughed, quietly.

"What is it," Cindy asked.

"I haven't laughed in more than a month," Julia said.

Cindy put her arms around Julia and pulled her in an embrace. "Oh, honey, I'm so sorry," Cindy said, as she held her for several minutes. Finally, they separated. "We'd better get going. Somebody probably knows we're gone by now."

Jericho

The sky threatened rain as Leah, John and Ethyl Abernathy, the Reverend E.D. Owen, Fred Bell, and Sheriff O'Shea gathered in the cemetery. The undertaker stood off to one side with the wagon that had brought the casket.

Fred Bell was wearing cuff restraints and Sheriff

O'Shea was there with him.

"Sheriff, thank you for allowing Fred to come to my father's burial," Leah said. "Papa thought a lot of Fred and he would have appreciated it."

"I'd more 'n likely have come even if I didn't have a prisoner to watch," Sheriff O'Shea said. "I thought well of Mr. Godfrey."

The grave had already been opened and a pile of dirt stood alongside the hole.

"Folks, if we don't want to get caught up in the rain, we need to get this done," Pastor Owen said.

"Can I say something first?" Fred asked.

The pastor looked at Leah, who was weeping silently. She nodded her approval and the pastor spoke to Fred.

"Keep it short, young man. I feel a storm coming."

The coffin had already been lowered and Fred stepped up to look down into the grave. He held his manacled hands out.

"They say that friendship isn't measured by the amount of time you've known someone, but by the amount of love in the time that you do know him. I wasn't privileged to know Mr. Godfrey for too long, but I did know him long enough to know that he was one of the finest men I ever met. I'm just sorry he's not going to be here to see Leah and me get married. Amen."

There was an audible gasp from Leah.

Fred looked toward Leah to see how she reacted to his comment and he saw shock in her face, but it didn't seem like a negative shock.

After Fred stepped away, the pastor began the grave-side committal.

"Forasmuch as it hath pleased Almighty God in His infinite wisdom and mercy to take out of this world the soul of our brother, Boston Godfrey, departed, we now commit his body to the ground, earth to earth, ashes to ashes, and dust to dust."

The preacher nodded at Leah, who dropped a handful of dirt. It made a sound as the dirt hit the coffin.

As the small gathering of mourners left the cemetery, the rain started to fall. Leah joined the Abernathy's and the pastor in the surrey.

"Sheriff, we're going to the café for dinner. I'd be obliged if you would let Mr. Bell attend. Of course, the invitation includes you," John said.

"Please, Sheriff, I would like that very much," Leah added.

O'Shea nodded. "All right, I don't know if that would hurt anything."

"Leah was with my daughter," John told the sheriff after the dinner was completed.

"You were with Julia Abernathy?" Sheriff O'Shea asked.

"Yes, sir."

"Well, where is she?"

"I don't know. We were separated, right before Fred and the Crocketts rescued me from King's men."

"The prisoner I have in jail now, Val Baker, says that Bell was with King. How could he come to rescue you if he was one of them?"

"He left King after the incident at the way station," Leah said. "He has been with my father and me ever since, until King came, killed my father and took me prisoner."

"When you say incident, are you talking about the train robbery?"

"There was no train robbery. King might have planned one, but it was prevented by Will and Gid Crockett."

"Where was Bell when King attempted to rob the train?" O'Shea asked.

"He was there."

"Did he fight against King?"

"No, nobody did. They were caught by such surprise that they weren't able to put up any fight at all."

"Baker says you were shot during the train robbery," Sheriff O'Shea said to Fred.

"I was shot, yes, but it's like Leah said, there really wasn't a train robbery," Bell said. "Two men were killed and then King 'n the others rode off."

"Still, you were there," Sheriff O'Shea said.

"I was there," Fred admitted.

"Not one shot was fired at any of the train crew or passengers and not one dollar was taken," Leah said. "Where was the crime?"

"That's for the judge to say. Come, Bell, it's time for us to get back," Sheriff O'Shea said.

"Sheriff, thank you for letting Fred attend the burial and come to the dinner. It meant a lot to me and I appreciate it."

"I'm just sorry there was such an event," Sheriff O'Shea said. "I'm proud to say that I knew your father and he was a fine man.

Salcedo:

When Will, Gid and Beans rode into town, the first thing they did was take their horses to the livery stable.

"Beans, how long has it been since you've had a beer?" Will asked.

"Oh, Lord, it's been a month o' Sundays," Beans answered.

"Looks like we won't have a hard time finding a saloon. Why don't you pick one out for us," Will said.

"Well, ain't you s'posed to be lookin' for somebody?" Beans asked.

"We are and the best place to get information is in a

saloon," Gid said.

Gid pointed to one of the saloons. "Well, the 'Brown Dirt' there says it serves food as well as beer. What do you gents think about that one?"

"Food is always good," Will said with a broad smile.

The three men pushed through the bat wing doors, then, to Bean's surprise, Will moved to the left and Gid moved to the right. The two men, with their backs to the wall, made a quick appraisal of the saloon. Then, after exchanging a glance, they moved back toward the center to flank a confused Beans.

"Why'd you do that?" Beans asked.

"It's just a habit," Will said without any more specific information.

The three stepped up to the bar and the bartender, after a quick swipe of the bar in front of them, looked up.

"What are you drinking?" he asked.

"Three beers," Will said.

"I'm told you serve food in here," Gid added.

"We do," the bartender replied setting up the three beers. "As good as any restaurant in town."

"We'll be at that table over there," Will said, pointing to an empty table near the back of the room.

The three men took a seat at the table and as soon as they were seated, Beans lifted his beer and had several gulps, didn't put the glass down until it was nearly empty.

"Oh, that was good," Beans said. "Most as good as coffee."

One of the saloon girls came over to the table. Although she was attractive, she wasn't as heavily made up, nor was she wearing revealing clothing like the other girls were.

"Ben said you gentlemen wanted food," the girl said.

"Do you have a menu?" Gid asked.

"No need for a menu, honey," the girl replied with a smile. "We only have one thing a day."

"What do you have today?"

"Roast pork, black-eyed peas, biscuits and gravy."

"All right, my friend and I will both have a plate," Will said, nodding toward a smiling Beans.

"And you, sir?"

"I'll take the same thing, only give me twice as much as you normally do."

The young woman looked confused. "Sir, I can't do that unless . . ."

"I'll pay for two meals, I just want both of them on one plate," Gid said.

The young woman smiled. "Yes, sir. I love a man with a good appetite."

"Miss, you have no idea what this man can eat!"

Kit Chiles started into the Brown Dirt but stopped when

he was startled by who he saw. There were three men having their lunch. He didn't know one of them, but he certainly knew the other two. They were the Crockett brothers. He remembered them from when they were tied to a tree in their encampment. He knew, also, that they were the ones who had sent Silas King to Huntsville.

What were they doing in Salcedo? Were they looking for him?

Chiles first instinct was to leave town, but he couldn't do that, he had to stay here until he heard from Abernathy.

He gave up the idea of having a drink in the Brown Dirt, but there were several other saloons. He purposely chose the Silver Spur Saloon, because it was the farthest one away from the Brown Dirt. Ordering a whiskey, he asked for the bottle, then took it over to an empty table so he could think. What should he do? He couldn't leave because he needed to be here to wait for the telegram. But if he stayed here, they were sure to see him.

Two more men came into the saloon at that moment and Chiles smiled. His problem was solved.

"Ed, Carl," he called. He held up his bottle of whisky. "Get yourselves a glass and come join me."

Ed and Carl were men he had played cards with over the last couple of evenings. Seeing the opportunity for a free drink, they each got an empty glass from the bartender and walked over to the table to join Chiles.

"When did you tell me you got out of Huntsville?" Chiles asked.

"About six months after you and King pulled your little trick," Ed said. "Only we didn't escape, we got let out early."

Carl laughed. "Yeah, I think they just couldn't stand to be around Ed anymore."

"Are you making any money?"

"Some," Carl said. "We got hired on at the Double Nickel ranch."

"Yeah, and that's just about what they's payin' us too," Ed said with a self-deprecating laugh.

"How would you like to make two hunnert 'n fifty dollars to split betwixt the two of you?"

"Who do we have to kill?" Ed asked with a little laugh.

"Funny you would ask that," Chiles replied.

Chapter Twenty-six

On the McKittrick Creek Road

The sun was warm, the rocking of the surrey gentle and the clopping of the horse's hooves almost musical. The result was that the two women often dozed, most often one at a time but both dozed more frequently than either thought was a good idea.

"Let's talk," Cindy said. "Maybe it will keep us awake."

"All right, you go first."

Cindy was quiet for a moment, before she spoke. "All right, my name isn't Cindy; my real name is Mary Beth Collins. I'm from Memphis, Tennessee, and I am..." Mary Beth paused for a moment then continued with a voice that was choked. "I *was* a school teacher."

"You were a school teacher?" Julia asked in surprise. "How did you become, I mean, how did ...?"

"How did I become a whore?"

"I'm sorry, I didn't mean to embarrass you."

"Oh, honey it's way too late for me to be embarrassed." Cindy continued the story, telling of being forcibly raped by her mother's brother.

"Neither my mother nor my father believed me," she said. "And my Uncle Enoch thought that gave him permission to have his way with me anytime he wanted. So, I left home. For a while, I tried getting a teaching job, but they wanted someone from Memphis to vouch for me, but by that time, everybody knew why I left. Thank you, Uncle Enoch." Cindy was quiet for a while. "Anyway, I finally got a job as a cook in a saloon, but the bartender forced himself on me and, somewhere along the line I just figured I may as well be paid for it. And that, child, is how I wound up on the line."

Although Cindy was using two hands to drive the surrey, Julia reached out to take her hand.

"You are a good person, Cin … I mean Mary Beth. As good a person as I've ever met. Have you ever thought about going back to Memphis?"

"I do worry about my little sister. She's about your age," she added. "I do miss her and I hope what happened to me doesn't happen to her."

"Now you must tell your story," Cindy said with a smile.

"Before I start, do you mind if I call you Mary Beth from now on?" Julia asked.

Cindy smiled. "I like that. From now on, I'm Mary Beth Collins again."

For the next hour, Julia told Mary Beth everything she could think of about her parents, the ranch, her room, even her Aunt Martha. She did not mention her indiscretion with Jamie Kincaid. It was as if she thought if she didn't talk about it, she could wipe it away.

Mary Beth stopped when they came to what looked like a trail leading off from the McKittrick Creek Road. "I'm not sure but I think if we go this way, it's about twenty miles to a town," Mary Beth said. She laughed. "And I'm not even sure what the name of it is."

"Whatever it is I hope they'll have a restaurant and maybe a telegraph station," Julia said. "I can send a telegram to my father and he'll come get us."

"Us?"

Julia smiled at Mary Beth. "Of course, I mean us. You helped me escape and I'm sure Papa will give you a big reward."

"Oh, honey, I'm not doing this for a reward," Mary Beth said.

"I know you're not. The reward is my idea."

Both of them heard the sound at the same time, the

thunder of hoofbeats. Turning, they saw two horses coming at a gallop.

"It's King!" Julia said in a frightened voice. "Oh, and it's Jamie!"

Mary Beth slapped the reins against the back of the horse and it went from an easy trot, to an all-out gallop.

The front wheel was whirling so fast that the spokes were a blur and Julia held on to her seat as Mary Beth controlled the horse.

From time to time Julia looked back and she could see that King and Kincaid were closing the distance between them.

"Oh, Mary Beth, they're gaining on us!" Julia said in a frightened voice. "Go faster!"

"Lancelot can't go any faster."

Mary Beth tried to get the horse to run faster but her response to Julia had been correct. Lancelot was galloping as fast as he could.

Gradually the two in pursuit came up on them and separating, moved up to either side of the surrey. They had guns in their hands and for a moment, Julia thought she was going to be shot. Instead, they moved up alongside the horse and pointed their guns at him.

"No!" Mary Beth screamed in horror.

Both men fired and Lancelot went down so quickly that the surrey was upset and both Julia and Mary Beth were thrown out.

Julia hit the ground hard and rolled a few times. She lay there for a moment, wondering if any bones had been broken. A quick glance toward Mary Beth showed her regaining her feet, and a moment later Julia was on her feet as well walking toward King who had dismounted.

King, who was holding a rider's quirt he stood there with the handle in his right hand, playing with the lash in the other.

"I'll teach you two bitches to run away from me," King said, angrily. "Kincaid, stand 'em up by the surrey."

"No!" Mary Beth shouted. "There's no need for you to go after Julia. She didn't have anything to do with this. I took her against her will."

"You took her? What the hell were you going to do with her?" King asked.

"I was going to do the same thing you were. I was going to ransom her back to her father."

An evil smile spread across King's face. "Well then, I guess I'll just have to punish you for tryin' to steal from me, won't I? Let me see her backside, Kincaid."

Kincaid stepped up behind Mary Beth, ripped down the buttons at the back of her dress, then cut her camisole so that her back was bare.

King swung his quirt at her and though Mary Beth didn't cry out, Julia did.

King continued to lash out at her and though Mary Beth could no longer remain silent, she reflected her pain with no more than quiet grunts. Julia wasn't quiet though and, with every stroke of the quirt, she begged for them to quit.

Finally, when Mary Beth's back was crisscrossed with bloody streaks, King, now winded, stopped whipping her and stood there, breathing hard.

"I'm goin' to stop here, while you're still strong enough to walk. Get a rope on both of 'em, Kincaid. We're goin' to take 'em back."

Kincaid took a rope down from their two horses, then dropped a loop around each of the women. He handed Mary Beth's rope to King and he kept Julia's himself.

"Let's go," King said as he swung into his saddle. "It's gonna be a long walk back to Diablo."

"Why did you say that?" Julia said, as she moved closer to Mary Beth. "Why did you tell them you were taking me against my will?"

"Why not?" Mary Beth replied. "He was going to beat me anyway, why let him beat you too?"

"You are the best, friend I've ever had."

"Julia, I know you're saying this because of the circumstances, but you don't know how good that makes me feel."

Chapter Twenty-seven

Salcedo

When Ed Potter and Carl Rathjen stepped into the
Brown Dirt, they saw three men sitting at a table that was
somewhat separated from the others. Chiles hadn't said
anything about a third man, but Ed and Carl were pretty
sure that two of the three men were the ones they were
looking for. The third man was older than the other two,
with white hair and a long white beard. But the younger
two fit the description Chiles had given them. One was
a big man, the other was smaller, just as Chiles had said.

"What about that old fart?" Ed asked.

"Nothin' about him, he ain't even wearin' a gun. We're
gettin' paid to kill them two brothers, 'n I ain't goin' to
kill nobody without I get paid for it," Carl said.

"Which one do you want?" Ed asked.

"I'll take the big 'un."

Beans had seen the two men come in and noticed that they were talking together without advancing farther into the saloon. He also saw that they seemed to be paying an inordinate amount of attention to this one table. They separated, one walked toward the back of the room, the other to the front. They kept their eyes on Will and Gid all the while and there was something about them that gave Beans some pause.

"Fellers, there's two men just come in that . . ."

"Thanks, Beans, I see 'em," Will said. "Gid, you keep an eye on the one behind me, I'll take the one behind you."

Gid nodded.

"Draw, Crocketts!" Potter shouted. He was behind Will and Rathjen was behind Gid. The two men already had their guns in their hands.

Without standing, Will drew his pistol and shot across the table. The bullet hit Rathjen in the center of his chest and an expression of surprise and pain twisted his face, just before he went down. At the same time Will was shooting Rathjen, Gid was shooting Potter and because he hit Ed in the center of his forehead, Ed didn't have time to be surprised.

Not until now did the brothers stand and they did so, with their hands still wrapped around their Colt .44s. The two made a practiced sweep of the room. All they saw were a handful of faces registering shock at what had just happened.

"I see nothing," Will said, quietly.

"Clear, here," Gid said.

Will and Gid sat back down and resumed eating.

"That's it?" one of the other saloon patrons asked. "You kill two people and you just go back to eating?"

"I was hungry before the shooting started and I'm still hungry," Gid said.

As Will, Gid and Beans continued their meal, the other patrons gathered around the two bodies.

"Anybody know these men?" someone asked.

"I've seen 'em around a few times, but I don't know their names or nothin'," one of the men said.

"That there'n is Ed Potter," one knowledgeable patron said. "'N that'n over there is Carl Rathjen. They both of 'em just come outta prison not more 'n, oh, a month or so ago."

"How is it you're a' know'n 'em, Muley? You ain't never said nothin' 'bout 'em before."

"They both of 'em was workin' out to the Double Nickell. Fact is, I got 'em their jobs."

"How come you was to vouch for 'em, not knowin' nothin' about 'em, or who they was 'n all."

"I know'd 'em," Muley said. "For a while, me 'n them was travelin' together."

The county sheriff had no deputy officers in Salcedo, but Salcedo did have a city marshal and having heard the gunfire he came hurrying in, with his pistol drawn. He saw two men lying on the floor and the patrons of the saloon divided into two groups, looking down at the two bodies. The marshal also noticed three men sitting at a table, eating, as if not interested in the two bodies.

As nobody was holding a gun, the marshal holstered his.

"Anybody want to tell me what happened here?"

"You should 'a seen it, Marshal. Them two fellers already had their guns drawed 'n was fixin' to shoot them two that's sittin' there eatin', but they got shot their ownselves."

"Which two?" the marshal asked. "There's three men eating at that table."

Will and Gid, without looking up, and without interrupting their eating, held a hand up. "That would be us," Will called out.

"What brought on the killin'?" the marshal asked.

"Well, I've never seen these two men before but it would be my guess that this had something to do with Silas King," Will said.

"Silas King, the outlaw?"

"Yes."

"Why would he be after you?"

"I expect it's because we're after him."

"Bounty hunters, are you?" the marshal asked, with a derisive tone of voice.

"Well, we won't turn down the bounty when we catch up to the son of a bitch, but that's not the main reason we're after King."

"And what reason would that be?"

"He's holding a sixteen-year-old girl for ransom. We've been sent by her pa to get her back."

The marshal nodded.

Will, Gid and Beans went back to their eating as the marshal moved around the saloon questioning the witnesses. Every witness, even including the bar girls, told the same story. Ed Potter and Carl Rathjen had attempted to kill the two men sitting at the table and they had shot in self-defense.

As Marshal Moore was talking to the witnesses, Hodge Carmack, the undertaker, came in with two helpers.

"Is it all right if I move the bodies, Marshal?" Carmack asked.

"Yes, I've seen all I need to see here," Marshal Moore said.

"What about us, Marshal? Are we free to go?" Will asked.

"Yeah, I don't see no reason to be holdin' you," the marshal replied.

"Where is it, we're a' goin'?" Beans asked, after they left the saloon.

"First place we're going is the barber shop. You're going to get a bath, a haircut and a beard trim."

"No, now I don't need no bath," Beans complained. "I had me one warn't no more 'n a month ago. 'Course, I didn't have no soap, but I splashed around in the water some."

"Will, if he takes a bath and gets back into the same filthy, ratty clothes, the bath won't do any good," Gid said.

"You're right, the first thing we need to do is buy him some new clothes."

Two hours later, Beans looked like a completely changed man. His hair and beard were neatly trimmed and he was clean so the only smell that came from him was the smell of soap. He was also wearing new clothes.

"It's been most a long time since I've changed clothes," Beans said. He wore a big smile as he ran his hand through his hair and across the front of his shirt. "I reckon that's why they said they'd more 'n likely burn my old clothes that I took off."

Both Will and Gid laughed.

"Now, the next place we're going is the livery," Will said. "We're going to buy you a new mule."

"No, now, I ain't goin' to let you do that. I ain't a' gettin' rid of Rhoda. Me 'n her is . . . well, she's more'n just a mule. She's my friend."

"Who said anything about getting rid of Rhoda? You can keep her, she just won't be working as hard," Gid said.

Three hours later, a cleaned up and well-dressed Beans, astride a new mule and leading Rhoda, with panniers filled with one hundred shotgun shells, bacon, beans, flour, sugar and coffee, was ready to return to his encampment. Sticking his hand down in his pocket, he felt the one hundred dollar bill his new friends had given him. It was the most money he had ever had at one time since he left the farm.

"You know what? Sharin' my campfire with you two is near 'bout the best thing I've ever done. I don't know how to thank you boys."

"You already did, when you warned us about those two coming toward our table," Gid said.

Beans smiled. "Yeah, well, I reckon that was a good deed on my part," he said. "If you two fellers are ever in need of another campfire 'n I'm anywhere close, drop by 'n I'll share it."

"As long as we have coffee?" Gid teased.

"As long as you have coffee," Beans replied with a smile. He slapped his legs against the sides of his mule. "Come on Ada, get goin'."

Will and Gid watched Beans ride away until he was well out of town.

"I'm sure he'll be all right," Gid said. "But you know what, in a way I sort of envy him. He doesn't have a care in the world."

Will laughed, then hit Gid on the arm. "Little brother, you'd go stark crazy if you didn't have somethin' to worry about."

"We should be worryin' more about Julia," Gid said.

"Yes, Julia."

Chapter Twenty-eight

Salcedo:

Shortly after Beans left, Will and Gid began to try and find out who had put the two men up to attacking them. They had never seen either one of them before and they were sure that the two had been paid by someone to come after them.

But who? If they could find that out, they would have a connection to Silas King and his gang.

They were in the Four Aces saloon when a smallish man with glasses and wearing a derby hat, approached them. "Mr. Crockett?"

"Yes, Mr. Jensen," Will answered, remembering the man who had sent the telegram to John Abernathy for them. "Do you have a message for us?"

"No, sir, but I've got something that may interest you.

I mean, especially after what happened this morning."

"What do you have?"

"Not long after you sent your telegram to Colonel Abernathy, someone else sent him one as well."

"Oh?" Will replied, his interest aroused. "Who was it, and what was the telegram?"

"I know the sender only by his initials, which I confess to finding a little strange," Jensen said. "But comparing the content of his message with the one you sent I . . . well, I'm not supposed to do this, you understand, but under the circumstances, I really think I should. Here is the telegram he sent."

FOUND LOST DAUGHTER WILL REUNITE WITH FAMILY COLLECT $20,000 REWARD RESPOND KC SALCEDO

"This is it! This has to be one of King's men," Gid said.

"Indeed it is," Will agreed. "Mr. Jensen, do you know how to get hold of this man?"

"No, but he has been checking in the office on a regular basis to see if there has been a reply."

"He just got one," Will said.

"No sir, we haven't heard yet."

"Yes, he has. I'll write one for you and you show it to him the next time he comes in."

"Oh, Mr. Crockett, I could never do that. Why, that violates just about every rule there is," Jensen said.

"You already violated the rules by showing me this telegram, didn't you?" Will asked.

"Yes, sir, I suppose I did."

"Why did you do that?"

"Under the circumstances, I mean comparing the message you sent with the one that the other gentleman sent, I thought perhaps that might be sufficient justification for me to break the rules."

"You want justification? A young girl's life is at stake. Is that justification enough for you?" Gid asked. "If you help us, we can save her."

"But what if we actually do get a return telegram from Mr. Abernathy?"

"Keep it to yourself," Will said. "Let's go to your office and I'll write the message I want you to show KC, whoever that is."

"Will, we'd better not go to the office," Gid said. "If KC is one of King's men, he might see us."

"He's already seen us, Little Brother. Why do you think he sent those two men after us?"

"If you don't mind me butting in, your brother is right," Jensen said.

"KC has made several visits to the telegraph office and I've no doubt he's keeping an eye on it. If you intend to make up a telegram, it might be best that you not be seen around the office."

"Yeah," Will said, seeing the validity of their argument. "All right, I'll write it here if I can find paper and pencil."

Jensen smiled. "I'm a telegrapher for Western Union. I'm never without pencil and paper."

Will took the piece of paper from Jensen, then wrote the telegram he wanted to be shown to KC.

AGREE TO TERMS MAKE ARRANGEMENTS FOR DAUGHTER IMMEDIATE AWARDING OF MONEY

Jensen read the telegram, then nodded. "I'll do it," he said.

As it turned out, the loft of the livery barn afforded an excellent view of the telegraph station. Will and Gid were there less than half an hour when they saw someone that they both recognized.

"Kit Chiles," Gid said, speaking quietly even though there was some distance between them and the Western Union office. Their horses were in the two farthermost stalls, already saddled, so there would be no delay in following Chiles, once he left.

Chapter Twenty-nine

Jensen waited nervously in the telegraph office. The real message from John had arrived a few minutes earlier but he knew it would not be the message KC was looking for.

MUST HAVE PROOF THAT YOU HAVE DAUGHTER. TO VERIFY ASK WHAT HAPPENED TO SUZIE

He was torn. Should he give KC the real telegram, or the one that Will Crockett had written for him? He knew what he should do but, as Crockett had pointed out and as was obvious from the exchange of telegrams, a young girl's life was at stake.

He put all doubts aside. He would show KC the false telegram.

His internal debate ended when KC came into the office.

"You got 'nything back from John?" he asked.

Jensen forced a smile. "Indeed I do sir," he said, handing over the telegram Will Crockett had written.

Chiles read it, then a big smile broke out on his face. "Ya hoo!" he said. "Wait 'till I show 'em this."

"I'm glad you're pleased with it, sir."

"Pleased? You're damn right I'm pleased."

"There he is," Will said when he saw Chiles leave the telegraph office.

"Looks like he's comin' this way," Gid said.

"Yes, I'm sure he has his horse stabled here."

The two brothers watched as Chiles came to the stable, his fast walk just below a run. At one time he pumped his fist into the air, the yellow message clutched in his hand.

Chiles came into the livery and the two brothers changed their position in the loft so they could observe him as he saddled his horse and prepared to leave.

"Snake, this here's what we was waitin' for," Chiles said aloud, speaking to his horse. "Yes, sir, me 'n you's about to be rich." Chiles chuckled. "Well, you ain't exactly goin' to be rich, but you ain't nothin' but a horse, so money don't mean nothin' to you."

Chiles threw the saddle on the horse and rode out of the barn.

"Let's go," Gid urged.

"Not yet," Will cautioned. "Let's let him get far enough ahead that he won't see us. The most important thing to do now is just see which way he's going so we can follow him."

"Looks like he's going north," Gid said.

"Then north it is."

The two climbed down from the livery loft, then led their horses out of their stalls and into the aisle.

Gid mounted first, and Will was about to, when he saw something in the dirt.

"Gid, look at this," Will urged, pointing to the ground.

"What is it?"

"These are his tracks. Look at that shoe."

Gid dismounted so he could get a closer look. "Is that him?"

"He had to come this way to get out of the barn and these tracks are fresh, no more than a couple of minutes old."

"I'll be damn," Gid said with a happy grin. "A tie-bar shoe. Why, Big Brother, he might as well be dropping bread crumbs."

"Huh, uh," Will said, his smile matching Gid's. "This is better than bread crumbs. Birds could come down and eat the bread crumbs. There's nothing short of a heavy rainfall that'll take this trail away."

Will mounted as well and they started north in trail of the man that they now knew was Kit Chiles. They could see him far in the distance, too far away to identify which meant if he saw them, he wouldn't know who they were. Also, this road was frequently traveled, so even if he saw someone behind him, he wouldn't immediately identify anyone.

"Let's drop back a little farther," Will suggested. "We won't lose him."

They continued to trail Chiles, not by sight, but by tracking the tie-bar shoe and saw that he had turned into McKittrick canyon, following the creek.

By mid-afternoon, they realized that they were approaching a town.

"I didn't know there was town over here," Will said. "You got any idea what it might be?"

Gid shook his head. "I don't know of one in these parts."

"Well, we'll know where we are when we see the welcome sign."

There was no welcome sign and the two rode on into the settlement. Unlike most towns they had reason to visit, this town seemed to lack vitality. The single street was lined on both sides with buildings of weathered gray boards. The signs announcing the various businesses weren't large and gaudy as in most towns, but were small, unprofessionally painted and sometimes misspelled.

"Let's find the marshal's office," Will suggested and the two rode from one end of the street to the other without seeing any indication of the presence of a lawman.

"Will," Gid said as they started back down the street. "Look over there. Isn't that the horse Chiles was riding?"

Gid pointed to a horse that had a white splash under the saddle. The horse was tied to the hitch rail in front of a building that bore the small, hand-painted sign: *Two Bit Saloon*.

Mary Beth was sitting on the edge of her bed. It was the first time she had been able to wear a dress that covered her wounds. Julia was standing at the window looking down on the street when she saw them.

"Oh!" she said loudly. "Oh, it's them! Mary Beth, it's them!"

"It's who?"

"It's Will and Gid. They've found me. Oh, Mary Beth they've come to get me!"

Julia started to lift the window and call out to them, but Mary Beth stopped her. "No! If it's your friends and they're here for you, don't give them away. Let them go about their business."

Downstairs, Chiles had just given the telegram to King. "All we got to do is set up the place where we turn the girl over for twenty thousand dollars," Chiles was saying excitedly. "'N they's only three of us to divide it up."

"Two of us," King said.

"What do you mean, two of us? They's Kincaid, too. I mean, he's the one that brung the girl to us in the first place."

"I'm takin' ten thousand dollars," King said. "If you want to give him half of your half, go ahead."

Chiles glanced over at Kincaid, who at that moment was signaling one of the girls to come to him.

"Hey, Roxie, how 'bout a poke?" Kincaid asked when the girl approached.

Because Kincaid seemed to be flush with money, he could have any of the girls at a mere beckon and Roxie felt pleased about being the one he had chosen.

"All right, honey, let me go up first, then give me just a minute, then you come on up," Roxie said with a flirtatious smile.

Kincaid glanced over at King, who was standing at the bar with Chiles, and King nodded at him.

In front of the saloon, their arrival noticed by no one but Julia, Will and Gid looped the reins around the rail. Both men loosened their guns in their holsters, then with a nod toward each other, stepped into the saloon. They didn't bother to enter it the way they normally did, this time they just stepped right in and they saw King and Chiles standing at the bar.

"Mr. King, Mr. Chiles, we've come for the girl," Will announced. Neither Will nor Gid had yet drawn their guns.

"What the hell?" King shouted in surprise.

The room grew quiet.

"Either tell us where she is and surrender or draw your guns and die. It's your choice."

Because Kincaid had heard Will's challenge to King, he turned to look back down toward the bar and as a result, he hadn't noticed Julia at the head of the stairs.

"Will, Gid, I'm up here!" Julia shouted.

"Julia, get back," Will called.

Having heard Julia's shout, Kincaid reached back and grabbed her, then held his gun to her head.

"Well now," Kincaid shouted. "Looks to me like you two boys just stepped right in a pile of shit. Drop your guns, or I'll blow little Miss Abernathy's brains out."

"Good job, Kincaid!" King called, as he and Chiles drew their own guns.

"Now you two drop your guns, 'n we'll start this little party all over again, only this time, I'll be in control," King said.

The victorious smile on King's face was replaced by an expression of shock when the sound of a pistol shot filled the room. Fearing that Kincaid had shot Julia, Will looked toward the stairs, where he saw Kincaid tumbling over the railing with a bleeding hole in the back of his head. Now, in place of Kincaid standing there with Julia, it was a woman holding a smoking gun.

That gunshot was followed by another as Chiles fired at Will and Gid, his bullet crashing harmlessly through the front window. Gid and Will both drew and returned fire. Chiles fell forward with a bullet in his heart, King, who had been hit in the arm, dropped his pistol unfired.

"You got me," he shouted.

A quick perusal of the room showed nobody else had any interest in joining the fray.

Jericho - Three Weeks Later

The trial had been quick and efficient. For the murder of Mrs. Edna Turnbaugh, the customer in the bank of Commerce, Silas King was found guilty and sentenced to death by hanging.

For the murder of Boston Godfrey, Val Baker was found guilty and sentenced to death by hanging.

Because of his role in rescuing Leah Godfrey and also because he brought in the murderer, Val Baker, Fred Bell's participation in the aborted train robbery had been set aside and he was acquitted and released.

Any hanging would draw a crowd, but a double hanging was a rare enough event to draw spectators, not only from

Jericho, but from all over the county. There were at least two hundred people gathered in front of the gallows on First Street at nine o'clock of a Friday morning.

An enterprising vendor had set up a lemonade stand nearby and was doing a brisk business as the day grew warm under a cloudless sky. Women in the crowd fanned themselves. A few of the men had brought whisky to steel themselves for the event they were about to watch.

Will, Gid, Fred, Leah, John, Ethyl, Leo, Mary Beth and Julia were there. John and Ethyl had debated whether or not to allow a sixteen year old girl to attend a hanging, but reached the decision that Julia had already been subjected to so much from these men that she had every right to be there.

A preacher, seeing a captive audience, was standing on the floor of the gallows, passionately delivering a sermon that few were listening to.

"Here they come," someone said, and a buzz of excitement passed through the crowd as everyone turned to watch the gruesome procession. The two new deputies Sheriff O'Shea had recently hired were bringing the two condemned men, one in front and one behind. Silas King and Val Baker had their hands shackled behind their backs.

Sheriff O'Shea was waiting on the platform along with the preacher and the hangman. When the hangman positioned the two men, the sheriff stepped to the front of the platform and read the court order, condemning the two prisoners.

"Mr. Hangman, do your duty," O'Shea said after reading the court order.

"Do you want a hood, sir?" the hangman asked King.

"Why the hell would I want a hood? Will it keep the rope from breaking my neck?"

There was a nervous laughter from some of those close enough to have heard the exchange.

"Uh, no sir, of course not."

"Then quit the gabbing and get it done."

Epilogue

One year later

The sign in front of the building read: Eagle Spring Way Station and Bell Furniture.

Leah stepped out to meet the train and the conductor stepped down from one of the cars and approached her with a smile.

"Hello, Mrs. Bell. How are you doing this fine day?" Bill Gillespie asked.

"I couldn't be better."

Gillespie handed Leah an envelope. "I know I'm cheating the post office out of a penny, but Colonel Abernathy asked me to give you this."

"Why, thank you."

Leah read the note, smiled at its contents, but waited until the train had left before going into Fred's shop behind the way station. Fred and Ernie Conroy, his helper, were working on a large table.

"Sweetheart?" Leah said.

Fred looked up and with a happy smile, lay down his adz, then walked over toward her. "You know you aren't allowed in here without paying a toll," he said, leaning down to give her a quick kiss.

"We've been invited to dinner next Saturday."

"In Jericho?"

"No, at the Abernathys. He says he'll have someone meet us at the train, in Toyah."

"Are you sure you should be traveling?" Fred asked showing no enthusiasm.

"Will and Gid will be there," she said.

The lack of enthusiasm was replaced by an eager smile. "Yes!" he said. "It'll be great to see the Crocketts again."

When Fred and Leah stepped down from the train at the Toyah depot, they were met by Leo and Mary Beth Hunter.

"Mary Beth," Leah greeted. "Shouldn't you be teaching?"

"Julia is handling it today," Mary Beth said. "Ever since the colonel built a school for the ranch children, Julia has been helping me."

"It was good of him to build the school," Leo said. "Now, no more long wagon trips into Toyah every day."

"And it gave me a job," Mary Beth said.

"And me a wife," Leo added with a broad smile.

Fred helped the baggage handler get the luggage, which included an inlaid, half-round, six-drawer cabinet.

"What's this?" Leo asked as he hurried to help.

"Your wedding present," Fred said.

"Oh! I've never seen anything so beautiful!" Mary Beth said. "Thank you, Fred, thank you Leah, I don't know what to say."

"It is beautiful, isn't it?" Leah said. "I think it is some of Fred's finest work."

"Wait, you mean everything else I do isn't fine?" Fred teased.

"Sweetheart, I did say, 'some of his finest work' didn't I? That certainly doesn't limit your finest work to this one piece."

When they arrived at Long Trail, they were greeted not only by John and Ethyl, they were also greeted by Will and Gid.

"Ethyl has prepared a feast for us tonight," John said. "That's the only way I can say it. It is a feast."

Ethyl chuckled. "Maria has done the lion's share. Mary Beth, Julia and I helped where we could."

"So if you don't like it, don't blame us," Julia said quickly.

The others laughed.

"Will, Gid, what brings you here?" Fred asked.

"Isn't it enough that we have friends here?" Gid replied.

"We've been married for a year and you just now decide to come visit?"

"He's got us, there, Gid," Will said with a chuckle. "We're on our way back to Missouri to pick up some mules we'll be delivering to Ft. Yuma."

"I thought it might be something like that."

"So, Leah, dear, if you don't mind my asking, when is the baby due?" Ethyl asked.

"Not for another couple of months," Leah said.

"We've been in touch with Dr. Berry," Fred said. "Leah will go into town when the time comes."

Ethyl laughed. "Babies come on their own time schedule. But even if Leah doesn't get there in time, she'll be fine. I was all alone when Julia came."

"And don't think she hasn't reminded me of that a few times," Julia said.

The others laughed.

There were seven people gathered around the table, whereupon sat a roast beef cooked with carrots and potatoes, English peas, freshly baked bread and peach cobbler.

When all were seated, John bowed his head to give the blessing.

"Lord, we bless this food to our use and ourselves

to thy service. And Lord, we give special thanks to our friends Will and Gid, who have enriched us with the gift of prolonging the lives of our daughter, Julia and our friends, Mary Beth, Leah and Fred Bell. In the name of the Lord, amen.

There were six more amens.

If You Liked This, You Might Like:
Lou Prophet: The Complete Series,
Volume 1

THIS PROPHET IS RIDING TO HELL AND BACK.

Lou Prophet's life as a bounty hunter has taught him one rule: You don't stop riding till the job is finished. Prophet is repeatedly caught in bloody crossfires and he is determined to show the outlaws that justice doesn't always wear a badge.

Join the bounty hunter as he searches for a gorgeous showgirl, chases down a brutal gang, protects his partner at all costs, escorts a Russian noblewoman on an Arizona trail and captures stage-robbers!

"A storyteller who knows the West."—Bill Brooks

Lou Prophet: The Complete Series, Volume 1 includes – The Devil and Lou Prophet, Riding With the Devil's Mistress, The Devil Gets His Due, Staring Down the Devil, and The Devil's Lair.

AVAILABLE NOW ON AMAZON

If You Liked This, You Might Like:
Lou Prophet: The Complete Series
Volume 4

About the Author

Robert Vaughan sold his first book when he was 19. That was 57 years and nearly 500 books ago. He wrote the novelization for the mini-series Andersonville. Vaughan wrote, produced, and appeared in the History Channel documentary Vietnam Homecoming.

His books have hit the NYT bestseller list seven times. He has won the Spur Award, the PORGIE Award (Best Paperback Original), the Western Fictioneers Lifetime Achievement Award, received the Readwest President's Award for Excellence in Western Fiction, is a member of the American Writers Hall of Fame and is a Pulitzer Prize nominee.

Vaughan is also a retired army officer, helicopter pilot with three tours in Vietnam. And received the Distinguished Flying Cross, the Purple Heart, The Bronze Star with three oak leaf clusters, the Air Medal for valor with 35 oak leaf clusters, the Army Commendation Medal, the Meritorious Service Medal, and the Vietnamese Cross of Gallantry.